Kate had never paid much attention to her own body, never compared it with those of other women, because there had never been any need. Since she had no intention of loving anyone or sharing her life with him, she had had no need to look at her body in the light of its appeal to a man. Now she wondered whether Rick's stillness was caused by revulsion or amusement.

'What's wrong?' Rick demanded softly.

'Stop looking at me like that.'

'Like what?'

'Like I'm some kind of... of inferior specimen of my species.'

His head turned slightly and his glance locked with hers. 'Is that what you thought? You couldn't be more wrong.'

EQUAL OPPORTUNITIES

BY

PENNY JORDAN

MILLS & BOON LIMITED
ETON HOUSE   18-24 PARADISE ROAD
RICHMOND   SURREY   TW9 1SR

First published in Great Britain 1989
by Mills & Boon Limited

© Penny Jordan 1989

Australian copyright 1989
Philippine copyright 1989
This edition 1989

ISBN 0 263 76309 9

Set in Times Roman 10½ on 12¼ pt.
05-8907-50720 C

Made and printed in Great Britain

CHAPTER ONE

'WHAT exactly do you mean, it's too late to claim the child?'

David Wilder glanced apprehensively at his extremely grim client. He had been warned when he joined the prestigious city law firm of Rainer, McTeart and Holston that some of their clients were very demanding indeed, with exacting standards and sometimes very strong and unfortunately erroneous views about their rights under British law.

'Unfortunately we do number among our clients a few who do not yet seem to be aware that there are some things that money just cannot buy,' the senior partner had told him.

The senior partner was also his godfather, which was how he had come to join the practice in the first place; a relationship which he suspected was not going to protect him at all when the full wrath of the man standing opposite him burst upon his head.

He had acted for the best, he reflected miserably. A minor matter was how the senior partner had described the whole affair: something that need not concern their prestigious client, who was, in any event, out of the country on business at the time. Besides, the woman had already made it clear that she would take charge of the child. How was he supposed to know that Garrick Evans would want the child himself?

It was not, after all, as though there was anything other than the most tenuous of blood ties between them; the son of his deceased second cousin.

'What do you mean, it's too late?' Garrick Evans demanded, repeating his earlier question. The lowered volume of his voice in some odd way added to its menace.

He was a tall man, a good two inches over six foot, with a frame that reminded David Wilder of his school days and the torments of the rugby field. He himself was of a much slighter built, and he gave an inward shudder at the very hardness of the other man. Garrick Evans was well into his thirties, and yet there was an air of honed fitness about him that suggested that he did not spend all his time poring over balance sheets and negotiating deals. But to read the financial press one would think that he did.

"One of the most important power brokers of our time," was how the *Financial Times* had described him, and in doing so had coined a new phrase. A power broker was exactly what Garrick Evans was: a man whose skills in assessing the weak points of an institution and then turning them to either his own or his clients' advantage were so notorious that it was said in the city that whole boards quailed at the sound of his name.

A millionaire before he was thirty, he no longer spent his time buying and selling vast corporations, but instead used his skills on a consultancy basis, normally working for governments or very large corporations. He also gave a great deal of his time to ensuring the profitable running of several large charities—time which he gave free of charge, although very few people knew it.

Garrick Evans had learned a very long time ago that to show people a weakness was to invite them to take advantage of it.

David Wilder cleared his throat and looked nervously into the cold grey eyes of his client.

'Well...that is... Well, the fact is that by declaring that you were abdicating from any responsibility toward the child, you have also given up any rights you might have had over him.'

'*I?*' Garrick queried drily. 'Odd ... I don't seem to remember making such a momentous decision.'

'Well, no. You were out of the country at the time, in Venezuela, I believe. You may remember you had given strict instructions that you were only to be contacted in an emergency.'

'I see. And you, of course, didn't consider that the death of my cousin and his wife was an emergency. Is that it? Never mind the fact that my cousin has named me as co-guardian of his child.'

'He was only your second cousin,' David muttered helplessly. 'There had been no contact between you as far as we knew.'

He didn't add that the whole office knew of his well-documented loathing of hangers-on of any kind, and it was for that reason that David had assumed that he wouldn't want the child.

'So, there was an error of judgement. Now what we have to do is to correct that error. Have you been in touch with the woman? What's her name?'

'Kate Oakley,' David supplied for him, admitting, 'Well, no, not yet. We weren't sure what your instructions were going to be.' He cleared his throat nervously again. 'You see, it would be very difficult now to reclaim the child. We would have to prove negligence on the part of your co-guardian. And here, the mere fact that she's a woman, and you're a man, would immediately balance these scales in her favour... We could try to negotiate, of course.'

He said it so doubtfully that Garrick frowned.

'How much do you know about her?' he questioned abruptly.

Silently, David Wilder handed him a file.

'Let me read this and then I'll come back to you. In the meantime, don't do anything. If I think it necessary, I'll go and see Miss Oakley myself. It may be that I will be able to persuade her to see the advantages of the child's coming to me,' he said grimly.

A few hours later, when David Wilder was relating the story to his wife while she was preparing dinner, she turned her head and said thoughtfully, 'Buy her off, did he mean?'

David winced, but admitted that it was a strong possibility.

'Well, I hope she turns him down,' Elaine told him roundly. 'That poor baby... What on earth does he want it for, anyway? He doesn't strike me as a man who would want to take on such a responsibility. Heavens, he's never in one place long enough to bring up a child.'

'He wants an heir, I suppose,' David told her.

'Oh, I see, and rather than go to the trouble of finding himself a wife, he's decided he'd prefer to take on a ready-made son without the nuisance of a woman who might make emotional and financial demands on him. Typical! Just the sort of thing I would have expected from a man like him,' she said scathingly.

David patted his wife's hand, and put her outburst down to the fact that she herself was four months pregnant with their first child, a very emotional time for a woman, but of course there was a thread of truth in Elaine's argument.

Despite the fact that over the course of the years Garrick Evans had had several long-standing relationships with women, it was rumoured that he always made it plain to them that they could forget marriage. A hard man. A man it would be very difficult to get to know. A man who wore an air about him of always getting what he wanted. And what he now wanted was a nine-month-old boy, currently living with his guardian; a woman who, according to her file, was an orphan herself, without either wealth or family to support her.

Even if she wanted to keep the child, she would never be able to stand out against Garrick. Feeling rather sorry for her, David Wilder applied himself to his dinner.

Not all that very far away from the elegant terraced house which had been Elaine Wilder's parents' wedding gift to her and her husband, Kate Oakley sat cross-legged on her sitting-room floor, the telephone receiver jammed into the crook of her neck while she painted her nails with her free hand.

Her house, although not in as fashionable part of London as the Wilders', was every bit as elegantly decorated and furnished. As a PR consultant running

her own business, Kate was well aware of the importance of creating the right image; hence the nail polish.

She finished one hand and studied the effect with
a frown, while listening to her friend exclaiming in
amusement.

'Kate . . . you with a nine-month-old baby! This I
have to see. How in the world are you managing?'

'I'm not,' Kate told her firmly. 'That's why I'm
ringing you. In the last six weeks I've gone through
four supposed nannies, Camilla. It can't go on. I came
in tonight all set to go out to dinner with James, only
to discover the latest one waiting for me with her bags
packed.'

'Good heavens! Is the child so difficult, then?'

'No, not at all. If anything, he's inclined to be too
subdued. The shock of losing his parents, poor little
thing . . . No, the problem is me. Three nights this week,
I haven't managed to get in until gone ten at night.
Everyone the agency has sent me expects to work a
regulation seven-hour day; they don't like being alone
all the time with Michael; they don't like the fact that
I can't provide them with a private sitting-room and
a whole host of other luxuries, and as for their sal-
aries——' She gave a groan. 'The agency is starting
to do quite well, but not that well.'

She didn't want to tell Camilla what a struggle it
had been even for her to afford the new house. Up
until the arrival of small Michael into her life, she had
lived in a flat, but she had strong views on how a
child should live, and those did not include being
cooped up with no outside area to play in. The reason
she had bought this particular house had been because of its walled-in back garden.

Admittedly it wasn't very large, but it was certainly large enough for a small boy to vent his energy in. Of course, she was looking ahead. Michael was only nine months old, but in another couple of years...

'I see. I sympathise, my dear, but why have you come to me?'

'Oh, come on, Camilla. You know everyone there is to know in London. If anyone can help me, it's you. You must know where I can find a reliable nanny who isn't going to cost me the earth...'

It was so unusual for her friend to sound so exasperated that Camilla frowned and stopped doodling on her notepad.

She had known Kate for almost ten years. In fact, Kate had worked for her when she first came to London. Camilla had sold out her interest in her own PR firm several years ago, and now spent all her time helping her husband in his own business and looking after their twin daughters. She was proud of Kate's success and drive, feeling that she had been the one responsible for recognising and nurturing them, and she sympathised with her in her present dilemma.

She and her husband had only just returned from a six months' working visit to New York, and this was her first real opportunity to catch up with her friend's life.

'I think you'd better start at the beginning and tell me the whole story,' she suggested firmly. 'Apart from a frantic message on my answering machine, I know nothing whatsoever about this baby who suddenly seems to have taken over your life. He's not yours, of course...'

'No,' Kate agreed quietly, adding, 'He's my godson.'

Start at the beginning, Camilla had said, but she didn't want to. She had put those years at the orphanage and all the insecurities that went with them firmly behind her now, hadn't she?

'His parents were killed in a car crash. Neither of them had any close family.'

'No one? But, Kate, surely...'

'Alan has a second cousin, but they rarely met.' She said it in such a clipped voice that, even without seeing her, Camilla could sense her friend's reluctance to discuss what had happened. Kate could be like that at times, erecting fences behind which she quietly disappeared. They had known one another a long time, and yet Kate rarely talked about her past.

Camilla knew better than to press her now, saying merely, 'I see. So there's no question of you—er—handing over the responsibility of this baby to someone else?'

'No!' Kate told her explosively, and then, realising how much she had betrayed, felt obliged to explain reluctantly, 'I can't do that, Camilla...I can't explain it to you, but I feel I owe it to Jennifer, his mother, to bring Michael up myself. You see, I know she'd want him to have all the things that she and I didn't have. A real home life..she and I didn't have. A real home life...family...'

Abruptly Kate stopped. Already she had betrayed too much, revealed too much, and she started to shake a little as she clutched the receiver. This was the reason she hated to discuss the past: it opened up too many vulnerable areas, too many heartaches that had never properly healed.

'I see,' Camilla said compassionately. 'Well, my dear, there's only one way to do that, isn't there? You will have to find yourself a husband.'

There was a short silence, and then Kate said harshly, 'You know my views on marriage, Camilla. I'm a career woman who wants to earn her own security, not to receive it secondhand from a man who would walk out of my life whenever he chose.'

'Oh, Kate.' Camilla could have wept for her. Where did it come from, this deep, abiding fear of depending on anyone other than herself that made Kate so terrified of emotional commitment? Independence was fine, but it could be carried to extremes. 'Kate, marriage needn't be like that,' she protested quietly. 'Husband and wife can be equal partners, each loving and respecting the other... each mutually dependent on the other...'

'Perhaps,' Kate agreed after a long pause. 'But it isn't a risk I want to take.'

'Well, then, your next best alternative is to follow the example of someone like Britt Ekland, and hire a male nanny,' Camilla told her.

'A what?'

'A male nanny,' Camilla repeated patiently. 'They do exist, I promise you, and marvellous they are too, by all accounts. You'd be surprised how many single working mothers employ men to take care of their children, especially when they're boys. Male patterning and all that. And apparently it works. There's also the added advantage that there's less jealousy between Mum and nanny when she's a he, if you know what I mean. Less feeling that somehow or other someone else is taking your place with the baby.

Look, I know an agency that specialises in finding male nannies. Why don't I give them a ring on your behalf and see what they can come up with?' she suggested.

A *male nanny*! Kate frowned. Did she really want a strange young man sharing her home? And yet the suggestion had its good points. She had been conscious of rather more than mere covert disapproval from a couple of the girls she had been employing, as though they felt that she was somehow not doing her best for Michael by going out to work, and yet what alternative had she? If she didn't work, she could not support herself. She had no money, no family, nothing to fall back on other than her own skills in the workplace.

'Look, give it a try,' Camilla urged her. 'What have you got to lose? I'll give the agency a ring, get them to send someone round, and if you don't like them . . . Well, there's nothing lost, is there?'

'All right,'' Kate agreed hesitantly. From upstairs she caught the sound of a small, fretful wail. 'I'll have to go. Michael's just woken up.'

'OK. Leave everything to me. I'll sort something out. Oh, and by the way, how *are* you getting on with James?'

James Cameron owned, among other things, a chain of supermarkets spread throughout the country, and through Camilla's good offices Kate had got the opportunity to take over his PR work. The supermarkets, for one reason or another, did not have a good image, and if Kate could get the contract to change this it would be a very healthy boost to her profits.

'He's taking me out to dinner next week. I've got to prepare a couple of presentations for him. He wants to start going up-market with the supermarket acquisition.'

'Watch out for him, Kate,' Camilla warned. 'He regards himself as something of a stud.'

'Don't they all?' was Kate's grim response, and Camilla sighed at her tone of voice.

'Some do,' she admitted, 'but there are others. Men who like and respect women as well as desire them. The problem with you is that because you prefer to think that all men are like the Jameses of this world, you deliberately close your eyes to the existence of the other sort. I've often wondered why.'

'It's safer that way,' Kate told her, and then stopped abruptly. She was giving too much away. Betraying more about herself than was wise. Good friend though Camilla was, if she were to learn of Kate's fear of committing herself emotionally to someone, and through that commitment being hurt as she had been hurt as a child, Camilla would, for the very best of reasons, try to change her outlook. And she didn't want her outlook changing. She felt safer with it the way it was.

Their conversation over, she went upstairs and walked into Michael's bedroom, switching on the light. She had purposefully put a soft light in this room, so that no brightness would distress the baby.

Michael had been premature, and was still slightly small for his age. He was wide awake and not crying now that he saw her. As she reached down into the cot, he raised his arms to her.

Kate picked him up, and comforted him automatically. She felt the dampness of his mouth where he sucked her shoulder and her silk shirt. Damn! She normally changed when she got home from work, but tonight, what with the rumpus with the nanny, she hadn't had time.

He had thrown off his blankets and his hands felt cold. She reached down into the cot and picked one up, wrapping him securely in it. Thinking he was going to be put down, he started to cry, his small features puckering.

The social worker who had interviewed her following Alan and Jen's deaths had warned her that for some considerable time Michael was going to feel insecure. So far this insecurity had manifested itself in bouts of tears in the middle of the night which had necessitated Kate getting up to take the baby into her own room, while his nanny slept on, apparently undisturbed by the noise.

Years of living with small children had given Kate an expertise she had not even realised she possessed until Michael came into her life. She was half appalled by her own inherent skill in looking after him, at least physically. Emotionally, she wasn't anything like as sure that she would be able to cope with his needs.

She adjusted her stance to cope with his weight with an expertise that would have astounded most people who knew her, easily rocking her body so that its rhythm soothed his whimpers.

The tears had stopped now, but she knew from experience that the moment she tried to put him back in his cot they would start again; it was all too understandable, really, this defiant bid to claim her attention.

None of the nannies she had had so far had been pleased by her ruling that Michael was to remain upstairs. The house was only small, and the sitting-room and dining-room she had had so carefully furnished sometimes had to double as an extension of her office.

Clients sometimes visited her at home; she entertained them at small, elegant dinner parties, using the recipes she had carefully and meticulously learned at nightschool. She wasn't an inspired cook, but she had the intelligence to realise that every tiny skill she added to her repertoire increased her chances of ultimate success.

A male client, dubious about dealing with one of the new breed of city career woman, could have his fears soothed by the production of a delicious home-cooked meal, thus restoring his innate belief that women, even career women, enjoyed pandering to men. It was because she had to look upon her sitting-room and dining-room as extensions of her office that Michael was barred from them. A scatter of toys and baby things, no matter how domestic, would not serve to enhance the image she was careful to project.

Instead she had given Michael the largest of the three bedrooms, and what was more she had decorated it herself—another learned skill.

Nor could she simply abandon her responsibility to him. Jen had been as close to her as if they were sisters. Closer in some ways. And she owed it to her friend to do the very best she could for Michael.

It would be easier once he was old enough to go to school...once she had her business firmly established. Already it was doing well, but not well enough for her to be able to sit back and relax. She would just have to hope that Camilla came up with someone suitable.

Michael was asleep... Very gently she removed him from her shoulder and walked over to the cot. Before she got there, he was awake, blue eyes regarding her with solemn regard, the baby mouth starting to pucker.

'All right, you win,' Kate told him wryly. They had been through this routine several times before. So often, in fact, that it was beginning to become a habit.

Not that she actually minded. There was something quite soothing about working in Michael's room, at the desk that would one day be his, and he seemed to find her presence a calming influence. He didn't even seem to mind the desk-lamp she used to illuminate her work.

Holding him against her shoulder with one arm, she went downstairs for her briefcase. The final details of the plans she intended to put before James were inside it. It was still four days before their meeting, but she wanted to be sure she had everything right.

Back in Michael's room, she put him in his cot again. This time, as though he knew that he had won

and that she would stay, he closed his eyes
immediately.

Kate wasn't fooled. She knew the moment she attempted to leave the room they would be open again,
and he would start howling—that thin, fretful cry that
tore at the nerves and penetrated so tormentingly every
barrier raised against it.

She ought to be used to crying babies; after all,
there had been enough of them at the children's home.

She opened her briefcase and extracted her papers.

James Cameron's supermarkets were in the main
small stores in country towns—often shabby and run-
down, from the information she had received. She had
driven out to some of them to check on the location
and size, as well as reading the reports he had given
her, and she was going to suggest to him that, since
he could not compete with the huge nationwide retailers, in order to make his image more up-market,
he got away from the plate-glass-window image of
supermarkets and instead went for something cosier
and more countrified.

Bow windows with Georgian panes had been her
first thought, as this would immediately give both a
more up-market image and have a much warmer
appeal to the shopper. At the same time she intended
to recommend that, where his own lines of produce
were concerned, he had the packaging changed in line
with the slightly Victorian, country look of the stores.
She had experimented with mock-ups of labels and
packagings in a soft gingham check so that she could
show him what she had in mind.

A new advertising campaign in line with this would
all help to reinforce the new image. TV and radio slots

with voice-overs in a warm, male, countrified accent. Posters and magazine ads concentrating on the wholefood appeal of certain lines.

What she had in mind would mean a radical re-think on some of the major lines the stores stocked, but since this would only be in line with the current interest in additive free, more healthy food, Kate thought that the two-pronged attack would have an increased chance of success.

It was gone eleven o'clock when she finished working. Her head was starting to ache, because the lamp she was using was not really strong enough for close work, but she hesitated to illuminate the room too brightly in case it disturbed the sleeping baby.

As she put down her pen, she could hear him making small, snuffly noises in his sleep. Strange how accustomed her senses were to him already after only four weeks; so much so that one night the momentary absence of them had actually woken her and she had rushed into his room to discover he had turned over and was lying with his face pressed into the bedding. There had been no real danger of him suffocating but, nevertheless, she was glad that her senses had alerted her to the hazard.

When Jen had asked her to be his godmother, Kate had never dreamed of what was to come. Poor little boy. She was really no substitute at all for his real mother, but she *was* that mother's choice, and when he was old enough to understand she would make sure that he shared as many of her memories of Jen as he could.

She was only thankful that tomorrow was Saturday. Not that she normally took the day off. It had been her habit to go into the office and go through the week's work. The two girls who worked for her were very good. Conscientious and hardworking, but it was not their business, not their future, not their success or failure. She had enjoyed those oases of time alone in the elegant but minute offices in Knightsbridge that cost her the earth, but that were worth it because of the cachet they gave her business.

Industrialists were snobs when it came to whom they used to sell their products, as she had soon discovered. They liked using agencies with smart upper-class reputations, and Kate had been quick to forge her own contacts with the prestigious advertising agencies.

Camilla had helped her there. Her husband was on the board of one of London's most prestigious agencies, and through Camilla's good offices she had made several strong and very valuable contacts.

Yes Camilla had been a good friend to her, right from the start when she had taken her on fresh from university with nothing but her degree and her determination to recommend her.

She had enjoyed those years with Camilla, but once Camilla had taken the decision to commit herself to Hugo and their family, Kate had known it was only a matter of time before her friend sold out, and rather than become a small cog in what promised to be a very large wheel Kate had taken the decision to set up on her own.

It had been the right decision, she was sure of that. The *only* decision, but as an employee of someone else might she not have been freer to spend more time with Michael?

It wouldn't be for much longer. Another couple of years and she would have successfully established herself. Perhaps she could even then start working from home a couple of days a week. Right now that wasn't feasible. She didn't have a good enough reputation, but if she got this contract from James...

Another valuable introduction Camilla had given her.

Yes, she had much to thank Camilla for, and she would have even more if Camilla found her a suitable nanny, she acknowledged tiredly as she snapped off the light and tiptoed quietly out of the room.

CHAPTER TWO

OLD habits died hard, and it had been a firm rule of the children's home where Kate had been brought up that everyone got up at six-thirty.

Even now, when she could have stayed in bed, she found it impossible, and in consequence, however late her night, she was invariably wide awake at six-thirty the next day.

This Saturday was no exception, and as she lay in bed listening to Michael's burblings on the intercom, she reflected wryly on the days when all she had to do when she first got up in the morning was to organise herself for her pre-breakfast run. Now she didn't run, but what she did do, rain or shine, was to put Michael in his pushchair and walk him to the park, so that they could both enjoy the freshness of the new day.

The park was small and Victorian, with formal flowerbeds and trees. There was a muddy pond in the centre of it, normally deserted in the early morning, apart from one or two moth-eaten ducks, soliciting shamelessly for food.

This morning, as he did every morning, Michael showed his approval of their outing by clapping his hands and laughing happily while Kate zipped him into his ski-suit.

She herself had pulled on jeans and a sweatshirt. She had discovered within the first week of having

Michael that her pencil-slim designer skirts and silk shirts were not ideal wear around a very young child, and so she had been forced to go out and comb the chain-stores in search of something more sensible.

Half a dozen pairs of jeans, plus an assortment of sweatshirts, had been the ultimate answer. Knowing Michael's propensity for covering them both in sticky mess, she no longer wondered at most young mothers' apparent uniform of jeans and tops. Running a brush through her hair, she gathered it up in a ponytail and snapped a band round it, before pulling on her anorak.

It wasn't easy to manoeuvre the pushchair down the stone steps, but she had developed a knack for dealing with them now. The street was deserted and quite dark still, but that didn't bother Kate; she liked the solitude of the early morning city, when most of its inhabitants were still in bed.

In the park the ducks quacked in welcome, but she didn't do more than pause to watch them. The object of the exercise was not just fresh air for Michael, but physical exercise for her as well, and that involved pushing the pram briskly ten times round the park and then back home.

Once there, she would put Michael in his high chair and make them both breakfast. Michael would probably throw most of his on the floor, and she would be lucky if she could even manage to drink her coffee before it got cold.

She was a dedicated career woman, with precious little security, a huge mortgage, a very new business to develop and no one to rely on but herself. Add to that the fact that she was solely responsible for a nine-month-old baby, the very last kind of responsibility she had ever wanted, and it seemed incredible to Kate that she should feel so absurdly happy. So happy, in fact, that once they had finished their exercise and she was heading back to the house, she stopped to blow kisses into the pram, causing Michael to laugh delightedly, and the man watching her from the other side of the road to frown.

That must be the nanny, Garrick reflected, watching as Kate skilfully negotiated the steps and unlocked her front door.

He had come here on impulse, a little surprised to discover it was so close to his own apartment.

He had spent the previous evening studying the file David Wilder had given him. On the face of it there was no logical reason why Kate Oakley should refuse to hand the child over to him. She was a career woman first, second and third; that much was plain. The kind of woman who would never willingly saddle herself with a child, and he should know...

His mouth twisted bitterly as he remembered Francesca. He had met her when he was twenty-three, and a very naïve twenty-three he had been, too.

Fresh on the London scene and working for a firm of merchant bankers, he had met Francesca at a disco. They had dated for two months before they slept together. Although they had been the same age, it had disconcerted him to discover that her sexual experience was far greater than his own, but he had accepted it when she told him that she had had a previous long-standing relationship with someone else. A relationship that was now over.

Six months later they were engaged. Six weeks after that Francesca had married someone else.

It had been then that he discovered how much she had lied to him. There hadn't been any long-standing relationship with someone, just a series of very brief affairs with a good many someone elses . . . men in the main much older and wealthier than Francesca herself.

Calvin Harvey had been one of those previous lovers. A married man now divorced—an extremely wealthy, once married man, who now wanted as his second wife Garrick's fiancée. And Francesca hadn't hesitated.

'But surely you understand, darling,' she had pouted when Garrick, white-faced and disbelieving, had finally realised that she meant what she was saying. 'It was fun with you and me, but marriage . . . Honestly, darling, can you see me as the wife of a poor man?'

'I wanted you to be the mother of my children,' Garrick had protested despairingly. He could hear her laughter still. Shrill and acid.

'A mother? Oh, my poor dear Garrick, what an idiot you are! I shall *never* have children. Such a bore . . . and it ruins one's figure. Don't worry, darling, it needn't end between us. Calvin has business interests abroad and he's away an awful lot. I'll ring you.'

And so she had, but only once. By then he had realised the truth about her and he had told her in plain and blistering English exactly what she could do with her favours and her much-used body. It had given him some temporary relief to his heartache. What a fool man was that he could realise exactly what a woman was with his mind, and yet not stop wanting her with his body. But all that was behind him now.

It had left its scars, though. Hence his determination not to marry, and *his* desire to take charge of his second cousin's child.

He himself had been an only child, but his mother had been baby mad. She had filled the house with the offspring of friends and neighbours. She and his father were retired now. They lived in Cornwall, where his mother painted and his father grew flowers.

He couldn't expect them to bring Michael up for him. He would need to find a reliable nanny. Perhaps even the girl that Kate Oakley employed. To judge from her behaviour, she seemed fond enough of the child. That shouldn't be too difficult... But he was running ahead of himself. First he had to speak with Kate Oakley.

He didn't anticipate having any problems, but he had learned long ago that it was as well to be prepared for all eventualities. If she should refuse to hand over the baby... well, then he would need all the ammunition he could find to prove that she was unfit to have the charge of him.

It had started to rain while he stood in the street, a fine November mizzle that soaked his thick black hair and made it curl. He hunched his shoulders against the damp, and wondered irately what had possessed David Wilder to behave so idiotically. Delegate...delegate...that was what he was always being told, and yet, the moment he did, look what happened!

An early morning cyclist braked to a startled halt as Garrick stepped out into the road in front of him, muttering under his breath.

Apologising grimly to him, Garrick crossed the road. He was thirty-five years old and a millionaire; once that had been said, what else was there to say? The woman who had been sharing his bed for the last three years had announced four months ago that the corporation that employed her was moving her out to New York. She would stay, she had intimated, if Garrick married her. He had told her crisply and incisively that he would not and why. And it had come as a slight shock to discover that he missed her sexually almost as little as he missed her emotionally...which was to say not at all. What was happening to him?

He knew the answer. Life had lost its bite, its savour, its challenge.

He had reached a time in his life when simply to succeed was not enough, and for some reason the thought of having a child, a cause, and perhaps at some later stage a companion as well as a successor, appealed tremendously to him.

Of course, he knew there were any number of women who would be only too pleased to give him a son. But that was not what he wanted. Their children would come with strings attached...demands, both pecuniary and emotional, which he had no wish to bear.

No, this child...this orphan would be ideal. And the child would benefit from their relationship, too. He would see to it. That Oakley woman would probably be all too pleased to give him up.

He now knew all there was to know about Kate Oakley, and he would use that information with all the ruthlessness for which he was so notorious, if he had to.

At eleven o'clock Kate's doorbell rang and she went to answer it, still wearing her sweatshirt and jeans. She and Michael had been building a tower of plastic blocks, and Camilla raised her eyebrows a little when Kate ushered her straight upstairs instead of into the sitting-room.

'Well . . . so this is the young man who's causing so much disruption, is it?' Camilla asked, swooping down on Michael and picking him up. 'Oh, he's gorgeous, Kate! Makes me feel all maternal inside . . . Oh, dear,' she laughed as Michael started to pout and turn his face away from her, holding out his arms to Kate.

With her hair in a ponytail and her face free of make-up, she looked closer to twenty than thirty, Camilla reflected, studying her covertly. At twenty-eight, Kate could still look absurdly young at times; watching her cuddle the little boy, Camilla wondered if she realised how expressive her face was. For a dedicated career woman, she was beginning to look surprisingly madonna-like. Wisely Camilla decided not to tell her so. She knew that Kate prided herself on her independence, and it wouldn't be kind to point out to her that that one illuminating smile had betrayed all too clearly how very dependent she already was on the small human body she was holding in her arms.

It was odd how kids got to you. Take her own two... She had vowed she didn't want any, and yet from the moment they were born they had turned her life upside-down and she had let them.

'Good news, I think,' she said cheerfully. 'I've found you a nanny. I got in touch with this friend of mine and she knows the ideal chap. Loads of experience. Adores kids and is especially good with young children. He can start straight away. In fact, the sooner the better. It seems that his previous boss started to get the wrong idea about their relationship, and propositioned him...' She gave a rich chuckle. 'It's good to know that sexual harrassment can work both ways, isn't it?'

Kate sat down, holding Michael on her knee. 'Camilla, I'm not sure about this... Perhaps when Michael's a bit older...'

The truth was that she didn't want to share her home with a man; she found the mere thought slightly intimidating, and yet, after all, what was there to be afraid of? She would be the one in control, she would be the boss... he would simply be her employee.

'Not sexual stereotyping, are we?' Camilla tutted archly, grinning at her. 'Men can take care of babies just as well as women, you know. Besides, I thought that we'd already agreed that a man would be best for you, less of a hassle for you to deal with.'

'Well, yes,' Kate admitted, remembering how much trouble her friend was going to on her behalf. 'But he'll have to live in.'

There was a small, surprised silence, and then Camilla said briskly, 'Well, you've got a spare room, haven't you?' adding firmly, 'Good heavens, Kate!

From what I've heard, this man is more likely to be terrified that *you're* going to rape him, rather than the other way around...if that is what's worrying you.'

'No, of course it isn't,' Kate told her testily. 'It's just... Well, I'm not used to sharing my home with a man.'

'No, you're not, are you?' Camilla agreed drily, and then reminded her, 'One day Michael's going to be a man, Kate, and quite honestly, for his sake...'

'Yes...yes, all right,' she agreed, giving in. 'How old is he, by the way?'

She was acutely conscious of how close she had come to making a fool of herself...of inviting Camilla to ask questions for which she had no answers.

'I'm not sure. Sue described him as mature. She says she can vouch for his references, by the way. In fact, she wanted to know all there was to know about you...which isn't a great deal. Apparently this isn't the first time she's had complaints from the men on her books about the—er—extra-curricular duties demanded by their female employers. It seems that there's more than meets the eye to employing a male nanny,' she added with a grin. 'Anyway, I've managed to convince her that you're not likely to demand your evil way with him, and so she's sending him round for an interview. Some time this weekend, but I'm not sure when. I thought I'd come round and alert you. As well as making this young man's acquaintance...' She paused to tickle Michael, who grinned back at her. 'Oh, and I explained to her that you couldn't afford to provide him with transport, etc., but she said not to worry, he has his own car.'

'Umm . . . It seems odd, though, don't you think?' Kate commented doubtfully. 'A man caring for a small child?'

'Not at all,' Camilla contradicted robustly. 'I know quite a few that do. Not professionally, perhaps, but I know a fair number of couples where it's the wife who has the career and the husband who's bringing up baby, and very well it works, too. Kate, do stop worrying,' she instructed kindly. 'If you don't like the man when you interview him, then simply send him away and we'll try and find someone else. All I can tell you is that Sue is very particular about who she has on her books, and according to her this man is one of her best. Mind you, you won't be able to look upon him as a permanent fixture, I'm afraid. She did also say that he's studying some kind of advanced computer course. Apparently he's worked abroad for some years and was made redundant. Now he's trying to re-train himself for the job market and earn himself a living at the same time. Hence the nannying. Look, I must go. I've got to collect the girls from their dancing class at one, and then we're taking them out for lunch. Oh, how about dinner some time next week?'

'I'll give you a ring if I may. After all, unless I get a nanny, I won't be going anywhere, never mind out to dinner,' Kate told her drily.

By the time Camilla left, Michael was grizzling for his lunch. Kate took him downstairs with her while she opened the fridge and removed the puréed soup she had already made.

Michael, sitting in his high chair, banged demandingly on the table with his spoon while she heated the soup. Already in four short weeks she had become dangerously attached to him; already she could see how he was changing, growing, and her heart ached for Jen and Alan. They had wanted Michael so much. Loved him so much.

After lunch Michael had a sleep while Kate got changed and did her hair. She had shopping to do, mainly food, but she liked to buy things that were as fresh as possible.

The rain had stopped, but the pavements were wet, and the air damply cold. Pulling on her trench coat, she checked that the safety harness was secure, and then manoeuvred the pushchair down the steps.

In the high street several men looked at her, admiring the slenderness of her ankles and the elegance of her high cheek-boned face. Her dark hair gleamed in the light from the shop windows, her immaculate make-up making several other women wonder how on earth she found the time to look so good, when she had a small child to take care of.

Despite the fact that her clothes were probably not much more expensive than those worn by her fellow shoppers, Kate stood out from the crowd. She shopped with the same brisk efficiency she brought to everything she did, quite prepared to haggle when she considered that what she was being offered was not value for money. She had learned in her early days in London to make her money stretch a long way. Not for her expensive and un-nutritious ready-made meals. She preferred to shop economically and make her own soups and stews, to search out the best bargains in fresh fruit and vegetables; frugal habits which she had maintained even though they were no longer strictly necessary.

It was almost five o'clock before she had finished her shopping. The streets were dark and damp. She paused outside a toy shop already decked out for Christmas. This would be Michael's first Christmas. She remembered Christmases at the children's home: busy, noisy affairs with presents bought and donated by various charities; church in the morning; then lunch and then a party at teatime.

Everyone had done their best, but Kate knew she hadn't been the only child there with a cold miserable place in its heart, mourning the Christmases that had once been.

Jen had once told her that she was lucky, because she at least had once had parents. She reached into the pram and touched Michael's face. He smiled back at her, and for a moment tears stung her eyes.

A woman of twenty-eight crying in the street—ridiculous. She straightened up firmly, but at the back of her mind lurked the knowledge that she mustn't fail Jen; she mustn't prove unworthy of the trust Jen had placed in her.

She had bought one of Michael's favourite treats for supper—bananas to which she added just the smallest spoonful of natural yoghurt. It was never too early to start teaching a child good eating habits, although she suspected that there would come a time when, like all children, Michael would insist on living for weeks on something like baked beans or fish fingers. Tea over, it was bathtime, a ritual which they both enjoyed, although it was only at weekends that Kate was able to share it with him.

One grim-faced nanny had complained to Kate that she didn't like little boys who made so much mess, and Kate, who wanted to encourage Michael to have as much enjoyment in life's simple pleasures as possible, had not been sorry to see her go.

This last one had been different; young and warm-hearted, she had seemed almost ideal. However, as she explained to Kate, her boyfriend did not like her having to work so many evenings, and so she had found another job which paid more and carried far less responsibility.

She was just preparing Michael's bath when the doorbell rang. Frowning over the unexpected interruption, Kate picked him off the bedroom floor and carried him downstairs with her.

Shielding him from the cold, she opened the front door. The man standing there was unfamiliar to her, and with the light behind him it was hard to pick out individual features. She saw that he was dressed in casual clothes; the streetlight shone faintly on the softness of a metallic grey leather blouson, and she also saw that he was very tall... tall and broad, with a silent, unmoving stance that was rather intimidating.

'Kate Oakley?' he asked her in a cool, firmly modulated, accentless voice, the words clipped and economical, as though he was a man who disliked waste, of either time or energy.

'Er—yes.' Kate stepped back into the hall automatically, and the man followed her inside, even though she had not invited him to do so.

'Let me introduce myself,' he began, and Kate's slight frown lifted as she realised who he must be.

'Oh, you're from the agency,' she interrupted. 'They did warn me that you would call round some time this weekend. Please come in... I'm just about to give Michael his bath. Would you like to come upstairs? We can talk up there. I don't like to disturb his routine too much.'

Without waiting for his response, Kate headed for the stairs.

Something about the man disturbed her. One look at those flint-hard grey eyes had sent her stomach churning with nervous tension, and she felt very much as though *she* were the one being interviewed, and not him.

He was older than she had imagined, too. Somewhere in his mid-thirties. Not at all the kind of man she imagined would want to spend his time taking care of a small child. But then, Camilla had warned her that he was simply working as a nanny while re-training for a new career.

She reached the top of the stairs and turned to look back at him. He was half-way up, and from her vantage point she could look down on the thick darkness of his head. His hair was well groomed and clean, his nails on the hand that held on to the banister well kept and shaped, but not the nails of a man who regularly visited a manicurist. His clothes were good and very expensive, she observed, noting the softness of his leather blouson and the way the dark trousers clung to his thighs. Italian and very probably cashmere. He must have bought them while he was working abroad and earning good money, she decided.

'The agency tells me that you're very experienced with small children,' she commented as she waited for him to join her. 'I must say I'm surprised.'

Three steps behind her on the stairs Garrick tensed briefly, glad that she couldn't see his face. What on earth was the woman talking about? And what did she mean—the agency?

Garrick wasn't used to being caught at a disadvantage, and within the space of ten minutes this woman had done so twice, even if she herself was not aware of it.

The first time had been when she opened the door and he had realised that the girl he had mistaken for the nanny was in fact Kate herself. All right, so now she had her hair caught up in an elegant knot, and he could see now that he was face to face with her the air of cool authority she wore. But he could also see how trustingly the child looked at her, and how competently she held him in her arms, as though she was both used and happy with his small weight there.

That knowledge disturbed him, alerting him to a range of possible problems he hadn't anticipated. What he had expected was that after a brief discussion he would offer Kate Oakley a generous sum of money to part with the child, which she would be only too relieved to accept, like the sensible businesswoman he had discovered she was. However, he was already beginning to suspect he had been too sanguine.

And what was this agency she was talking about? No one in the last ten years had ever mistaken Garrick for anything other than what he was: a singularly powerful and sometimes dangerous businessman.

'I know that the agency have vouched in full for your abilities, but I expect you'll appreciate that I'll have to ask you a few questions of my own. Did they explain to you that you'll be in full charge of Michael during the day? I work long hours, I'm afraid, and I don't get home until well into the evening some days, which means that you'll be on duty until I do return. Weekends you will be able to have off in full. I don't have a car, but the agency told me that you had your own transport. I'll show you your room in a moment. All right, Michael, I know you want your bath... I'm sorry about this,' she apologised to Garrick over her shoulder as she hurried into the nursery. 'But Michael loves his bath, and he's apt to get a bit impatient if the fun's delayed.'

She paused just inside the room, and said thoughtfully, 'Look, why don't I let *you* bathe him? As you will be in full charge of Michael, I'm sure you'll realise that it's important for me to feel that you can establish a rapport with him. I must confess when my friend suggested a male nanny, I was rather doubtful. She pointed out to me that Michael would benefit from the male influence in his life, but I feel he's rather young as yet for me to worry about male/female roles.'

Garrick, who had followed her into the room, stared at her back as she bent to put Michael down. Had he gone mad, or did this woman really believe that he had come here to be interviewed as a nanny for the child?

As Kate straightened up and gave him a coolly appraising smile, he realised that he hadn't, and that Kate did seriously believe that was why he was here.

He opened his mouth to correct her misapprehension, and then closed it again. Several times during his life he had been called upon to make split-second and impulsive decisions, and never once had his intuition failed him. This time it was telling him to go along with her self-deception. He was rapidly coming to the belief that there was no way Kate Oakley was going to calmly hand over the child. He could see just by watching her with him how fiercely protective of him she was. That in no way altered his own determination to have sole responsibility for Michael, but what it did alter was the method he would now need to adopt to get legal control of Michael.

David Wilder had warned him that the only way the courts would ever take Michael away from Kate Oakley would be if she could be proved to be an unfit guardian. And what better way to be able to prove that than to live here in the same house with them and to observe at first-hand how she responded to her responsibilities?

One set of facts could be presented in so many different ways, to give a hundred different impressions, Garrick knew that. He wondered what the courts would think of a woman who employed an unknown man to take care of a nine-month-old child without even making any attempt to check his credentials.

When Kate looked at him, he was smiling at her. It was an odd, chilling sort of smile, and for a moment she was tempted to snatch up Michael and tell him to leave.

Control yourself, she commanded inwardly. Just because the man is so much more . . . male than you anticipated, that's no reason to get in such a state.

But, as she watched Garrick remove his jacket and deftly roll up the sleeves of the shirt he was wearing, she couldn't help wishing that she had never listened to Camilla's suggestion that she hire a male nanny to take care of little Michael.

Bathe him, she had said, and Garrick thanked his lucky stars that his mother's preoccupation with infants had ensured that he had observed the bathtime routine often enough as a child and teenager to have retained some knowledge of what ought to be done.

Let's face it, Garrick told himself, Kate Oakley probably didn't have much more idea of how to take care of a small child than he did himself.

A dedicated career woman was how his data described her, and from the information he had been given he had formed the impression that she would be much harder, much, much more abrasive than she was turning out to be. Already he had discerned that there were certain anomalies about her... certain vulnerabilities that she tried desperately hard to conceal.

He took hold of Michael and started to undress him.

Kate watched impassively, but secretly just a little pleased, while Michael kicked and wriggled. The man didn't seem to be too familiar with the poppers on Michael's clothes, but his hands were gentle when he touched and held the little boy, she had to admit that, and she had to turn away from the sight of those male hands struggling with the small clothes. It brought back memories she wanted to suppress... memories of a time when she herself had been a much-loved part of a close family unit. A time before her world had been turned upside-down and her parents had left her . . . deserted her without any explanation, without any warning.

She noticed the faint grimace the man gave as he removed Michael's wet nappy, and suspected that she was probably right in thinking that he had never taken care of such a very young child before.

All her earlier doubts came sweeping back, and she stepped forward protectively, ready to snatch Michael away from him.

'I'm not sure that this is a good idea,' she said unsteadily. 'Michael is very young . . .'

She gave him a firmly dismissive smile and reached for her godson, but the man refused to let him go.

'Yes. He is small for his age, isn't he?' he agreed, deliberately misunderstanding her. 'Premature, was he?'

Garrick knew quite well that Michael had been premature, but he saw from Kate's face that his remark had startled her.

'Yes. Yes, he was a little,' she agreed reluctantly.

Without a word Garrick picked Michael up and carried him over to his waiting bath. Once there, he asked Kate over his shoulder, 'And his father . . . what part does he play in Michael's life?'

There was no harm in turning the screw just a little, he told himself, justifying his underhand actions with his conviction that Michael would be better off with him.

'Michael's parents are dead,' she told him quietly, the pallor of her skin making him feel uncomfortably guilty. He hadn't expected her to show such distress. He knew she had been close to Jennifer. The report had told him that much; they had, after all, grown up together in the children's home, but he had gained the impression from the report that she rather tended to keep people at an emotional distance, and he had formed the opinion that she would look upon the responsibility of Michael as an unwanted one. Now he wondered uneasily if he had been too sanguine in his assumptions.

To cover his own inner disquiet, he said quickly, 'So he isn't really your child, then?'

Not really hers! Kate caught her breath on an unsteady shock of tension, increased by her awareness of just how much she feared and resented the assumption behind the casual words. Michael *was* hers... When she thought of Michael, she thought of him as being her child, she recognised. She loved him, and not just because of Jen.

Panic bit into her... the kind of panic she always experienced at the thought of allowing anyone to come too close to her emotionally, but where Michael was concerned it was already too late.

She heard the man saying calmly, 'I'm sorry, I didn't mean to upset you.'

And she focused on him, her body as taut as a bow string as she fought off the feelings threatening her.

'You didn't,' she denied shortly, hoping he would drop the subject. To her dismay, he didn't.

'You must have been very close to the boy's parents. He doesn't look like you, though,' he added, looking first at her and then at Michael.

Kate drew a sharp breath, aching to simply demand that he leave. He had no right to ask her these questions, to pry into her life. And then she tried to control her reactions and remind herself that he was simply trying to do his job and that it was only natural that he should want to have as much information as possible about Michael.

Taking a deep breath, she said as calmly as she could, 'Michael isn't a blood relative. He's the child of a very close friend. She and her husband were killed in a motorway accident.'

'I'm sorry.' He wasn't looking at her now, whether out of compassion or simply by accident, she wasn't sure. 'It can't be easy for you . . . a single woman suddenly having a baby thrust into your life. Doesn't he have any family?'

He was probing too deeply now, but there was nothing she could do to stop him without betraying herself. She could feel the old, familiar tension building up inside her stomach. She wanted to tremble with the force of it, but she had long ago learned to control that reaction.

'Not really,' she told him shortly. 'Jen and I are . . . were both orphans. We grew up together in a children's home. Alan, Jen's husband, was an only child, his parents are dead, and I believe there is a distant family connection . . . a second cousin.'

'Orphans,' Garrick mused, ignoring the reference to himself. 'I see.'

Here was his chance to subtly undermine her self-confidence by pointing out that as an orphan she was hardly qualified to act as a substitute family to such a young child. . . to ask her if she didn't think Michael would be better off in the care of someone who could communicate to him through their own experiences, just what it meant to be part of a loving family.

Whatever else he might or might not be ... however cynical his views on marriage had become over the years, he could never doubt the happiness that his parents had had ... nor dismiss the love and security they had given him as a child.

It would be oh, so easy to make some idle comment that would increase the doubts he could see so clearly shadowing her eyes ... to reinforce what he was beginning to suspect was her own private fear that she was not an adequate parent for Michael, but to his own consternation he found that he simply could not do it. He was as amazed by the recognition of his weakness as he would have been to discover that the world had suddenly turned upside-down.

This couldn't be him, deliberately holding back on beginning his campaign to win Michael away from her, simply because he had looked into her eyes and seen the lonely, proud child she must once have been, fighting desperately to pretend that nothing was wrong ... that her world hadn't been destroyed ... that she wasn't....

He shook his head, wanting to dispel the unwanted images. What was happening to him? What was wrong with him? He must be going soft in the head.

'What's wrong?' Kate demanded suspiciously, her tension increasing as she sensed his hesitancy and knew instinctively that it had something to do with her.

'I was just thinking how very hard it must have been for you as a child,' he said quietly. 'And how much Michael must mean to you.'

Later he would ask himself what on earth had come over him, what on earth he had thought he was doing, but in the moment he said the words he saw the fury and panic fight for supremacy in Kate's eyes, and he reacted instinctively to them, reaching out his hand to touch her in an age-old gesture of comfort.

Even before he touched her, Kate froze, and immediately Garrick realised what he was doing and cursed himself under his breath. What the hell was happening to him? He must be going soft in the head, feeling sorry for her.

A nanny... God, he could just imagine what the press would do to him if they ever found out!

CHAPTER THREE

SEVERAL miles away, Camilla listened anxiously to the telephone call between her husband and his mother.

'Dad's been rushed into hospital with a suspected heart attack,' he told her as he hung up. 'Mum wants us to go down.'

'I'll pack a couple of overnight bags and we can leave straight away.'

Camilla loved her mother-in-law, but knew that she was quite incapable of dealing with an emergency.

It wouldn't be for several hours that she remembered that she had never told Kate that Sue had rung to say Peter Ericson had already accepted a post with someone else. She would do her best to find a suitable alternative, she had promised, but men willing to take charge of small children were not easy to find.

Kate, meanwhile, in blissful ignorance, watched as Garrick bathed Michael. It was true that he was less skilled than the other nannies she had employed, but his lack of expertise was more than made up for in the way that Michael responded to him.

Perhaps she had been wrong, she reflected, watching them, perhaps it was possible, after all, for even such a small baby to miss a male influence in his life. Michael, normally wary with strangers, was laughing and clapping his hands as Garrick bathed him, dunking his toys, and generally behaving as though there was nothing he wanted more than to keep on playing with this man who had come to take care of him.

The bath had its own stand, but Kate preferred to put it on the floor, for reasons of safety. She also normally armed herself with protective clothing, knowing Michael's propensity for soaking everything and everyone around him with water.

By the time Garrick had managed to fish Michael's wriggling wet body out of the bath, he was almost as wet as the small child.

As he handed Michael over to Kate, after swaddling him in a warm towel, he asked directly. 'First question. Do I get the job?'

He had removed his watch while he bathed Michael, and observing him strapping it on, Kate noticed that it was an expensive gold model that she knew must have cost several thousand pounds. Rather a luxury for a man who was prepared to work for less than a hundred pounds per week, all found. But then, perhaps he had bought it in better times, when he worked abroad.

She hesitated, and he gave her a frowning look. At that moment Michael managed to free his arms from the towel and stretched out towards him. Kate made up her mind, praying that she wouldn't regret it.

'Yes. Yes ... you do,' she agreed firmly, adding, 'What was your next question?'

'Do you have a dryer so that I can dry my shirt, and will it be OK if I bring my computer terminal with me?'

'Your what?' And then Kate remembered that he was re-training. Presumably he wanted to work on the computer in his off-duty time. 'Oh, yes. I don't see why not. There's a desk in the room. I'll show you. Unfortunately, though, it doesn't have its own bathroom. There is a bathroom here off Michael's room, but there's no bath—only a shower. The other bathroom is off my room, and...' She broke off, remembering what Camilla had said about his previous employer.

He had been direct with her, and in the circumstances she felt she was entitled to be direct with him. After all, she was employing him, although, looking at him, she found it very hard to believe that any woman was capable of sexually intimidating him... even when that woman was paying his wages. In fact, the more she studied him, the more astounded she was that any woman would ever dare to make unwanted sexual approaches to him. He struck her as very much the kind of man who wanted to be in control of his own life and everything and everyone in it.

Garrick waited, wondering what on earth it was she wanted to say to him. He wondered if she realised how very illuminating her expression could be, and suspected not.

'I know... I know all about the problems you had with your previous employer,' Kate said at last. 'And I just wanted to assure you that there is no question of them being repeated here.'

Garrick stared at her, wondering what on earth she was talking about. What kind of problems was he supposed to have encountered?

'Which problem in particular are we discussing?' he asked her silkily, surprised to see a dull flood of colour warm her skin. From her file he had assumed there could be little that had the potential to embarrass her, but it seemed he was wrong.

Was he deliberately being obtuse, Kate wondered angrily, or was he simply testing her to make sure he knew where he stood? She had a momentary desire to change her mind and dismiss him, but Michael had taken to him so well. He moved, and she couldn't help noticing the way the wet shirt clung to his chest. He must be anxious to get out of it; she knew from experience that there was nothing more unpleasant. Hastily averting her eyes, she said hurriedly, 'The problem of your ex-employer making...sexual advances to you.' She couldn't look at him, and so missed the stunned look that crossed his face.

Garrick didn't know whether to burst out laughing or pretend outraged male vanity. It happened, of course. He had been the victim of some very subtle forms of it himself, but he had never been in a situation where his livelihood depended on him acquiescing to the sexual favours being demanded of him.

He was looking at her in an extremely odd way, Kate realised as she raised her head, and it occurred to her that it might be that he didn't believe her. He was, after all, an extremely physically compelling man; a very male man...the kind of man, in fact, that many a single woman might fantasise about having as her lover. And many a not so single one as well, she acknowledged, giving him a covert glance.

His body had the kind of male power that promised all kinds of enticement and pleasure, if one was that way inclined, which she thankfully was not, but she didn't like the way he was looking at her, and so she rushed impulsively into an unplanned speech, saying quickly, 'I have no desire to have any kind of relationship, sexual or otherwise, with you or any other man. It's not part of my plan for my life.'

She had his attention now, but oddly he wasn't looking at her in the way that men normally looked at her when she made this statement. Indeed, if she had to define his expression, she would have had to describe it as faintly disapproving.

Garrick did disapprove—his immediate, almost emotional reaction to her statement, so surprising that he found himself forced to question it.

After all, she was perfectly free to live her life however she chose, and it was chauvinistic of him in the extreme to succumb to the wholly male feeling that in denying his sex any place in her life she was wasting the feminine gifts nature had given her. He was also angry with himself for allowing himself to think of her as a person, and not simply as an obstacle in his path.

Kate noticed the way he masked his expression, and a tiny inner voice warned her that here was a man it would never be easy to read.

'I see,' he said smoothly. Too smoothly? she wondered, uneasy without knowing why.

'And Michael . . . Surely he couldn't have been part of this life plan?'

Kate felt a surge of conflicting emotions. Anger that he had so easily found her weak point, and an uncomfortable, illogical dread that refused to be analysed.

'It can't be easy for you, a career woman, and single, presumably without any previous experience of child rearing, to take on the task of bringing up someone else's child. Wouldn't it have been easier to let the State take charge of him...'

Once again her expression betrayed her, although Kate herself wasn't aware of it. Without being able to stop herself, she said fiercely, 'I couldn't let that happen. Michael's mother was my closest friend. I....'

She broke off, and Garrick, realising that he was pushing too hard for a supposed employee, backed off a little, saying fake casually, 'Obviously nothing would make you give him up?'

'Nothing,' Kate agreed shortly, unaware that she was confirming his grimmest thoughts. 'You know I want to start work as soon as possible, don't you?' she asked him, changing the subject. 'Will that be a problem?'

'No,' he confirmed.

'And I'm afraid I don't seem to have your name as yet...'

'It's G...Rick...Rick Evans,' he told her calmly, watching her closely to see if she recognised the name. There was no reason why she should. Evans was a common enough surname, and there was no reason for her to connect Rick with Garrick, even though it had been his boyhood nickname.

He was right, she didn't. Kate was too busy worrying about whether she had made the right decision to wonder about that brief hesitation before he gave his name.

'I can start on Monday, if that's OK with you. I'll move my stuff in some time tomorrow evening.'

'Yes, that's fine. I'll show you your room. Oh, and your shirt...the dryer is in the kitchen.'

'Right. I'll take this off and put it in, if you don't mind.'

It wouldn't have mattered if she had, he was already removing it to reveal a hard, brown male chest so very powerfully muscled that she wondered where he did his exercising. The faint male scent of his body reached her and she stepped back automatically. Garrick, catching the reaction, was slightly surprised by it. His sexuality was something he had come to take for granted over the years, but it didn't normally elicit that kind of response from women.

Strange how her reaction had piqued his interest, making him aware of himself as a man in a way that he had not been for months. He hadn't missed having a woman in his bed, but that hesitant backward step, that covert look of apprehension laced with shock, that very definite reaction he had seen to her awareness of his male scent, caused him to suddenly become aware of the curves of her body, the narrowness of her waist and the rounded fullness of her breasts, so discreetly and tantalisingly covered by the softness of her silk shirt.

He liked silk on women, but a shirt like that should be worn without a bra underneath it so that . . .

'The room's this way.'

Grimly he followed her, subduing his wayward thoughts. They were neither timely nor necessary.

The room would have fitted into a small corner of his bedroom in his London apartment, but the desk seemed large enough to house a computer terminal. He was going to have one hell of a lot of work to do in the next twenty-four hours. For starters he was going to have to find a nanny to take charge of the boy during the day so that he could concentrate on his work. He would have to alert his secretary to re-route all his calls through his carphone. Luckily he was pretty clear of appointments. He would organise things so that Gerald didn't make any more... He could just imagine his impassive secretary's face when he announced what he was doing. Fortunately Gerald Oswald was the soul of discretion. He had been with Garrick for eight years and was completely loyal.

As to the rest, the fewer people knew what was going on, the better. It was just as well Kate worked long hours, he reflected grimly; the last thing he wanted was an employer who was going to pop home unexpectedly in the middle of the day. But somehow or other events were going to have to be engineered to prove that she was unfit to have charge of Michael.

None of what he was thinking showed on his face as he followed Kate downstairs, his damp shirt in one hand and his jacket in the other.

Michael was tucked up in his cot, apparently for once quite happy to go straight to sleep.

In the kitchen, while they waited for his shirt to dry, Kate showed him where she kept Michael's things and ran through the typed routine she had prepared for his previous nannies, handing him a copy.

'And if there are any problems?' Garrick asked her.

'In that case you'll have to ring me at my office... but only in the event of an emergency.' She saw his face and said defensively, 'I have a career, Rick. A career which I need in order to support Michael and myself, and so it's important that while I am at work I'm free to concentrate on it. That's why I'm employing you,' she reminded him sharply.

It was hot in the small kitchen with the dryer on, and she was acutely conscious of the bareness of his torso. She wished she could ask him to go and wait in the sitting-room, or to put on his jacket, but he would probably think she was mad if she did so. She still found it almost impossible to picture this man looking after children, but he had proved to her that he was capable of doing so. He had bathed Michael with a tenderness that none of his previous nannies had matched, and instinctively she knew that where Michael was concerned she could trust him implicitly. Where Michael was concerned . . . so was it then on her own behalf that she felt this vague feeling of disquiet, of . . . danger almost? And what kind of danger? Not sexual danger, surely?

No. Although he was a very sexual man; she was sure of it. His private life was no concern of hers, she reminded herself, and then her face flamed as it suddenly occurred to her that he might quite reasonably expect to entertain his friends here in her house. After all, her female nannies had expected that privilege.

The thought of him bringing a woman home with him and very probably making love with her aroused the most acute and unpleasant sensations inside Kate. She knew she ought to say something, to tell him that she couldn't permit him to do so, but she found she simply could not say the words. It was a problem she would have to deal with at a later date, she told herself, inwardly praying that the occasion would never arise, but all too aware that it most probably would.

The dryer stopped, buzzing its message of readiness. Before she could do so, Garrick reached behind her and opened the door. She moved in order to get out of his way, and instead found that she was trapped between his body and the dryer.

It was a nerve-racking sensation, although after he had gone and her pulse had returned to normal she wasn't able to understand why. He hadn't menaced her in any way, done anything, said anything to set off that sudden terrifying feminine reaction to his proximity. No...this fear was unique and hitherto completely outside her experience, and it was a fear of herself rather than of him...of her reaction, her arousal, her awareness rather than his.

Instinct aided her, making her lower her eyelashes to shield her eyes, making her tense and breathe shallowly until he had retrieved his shirt and put it on, making her avert her head so that she didn't have to look at him or breathe in his scent.

As she walked with him to the front door, she was half hoping that he would announce that he had changed his mind and had decided against working for her. She didn't want him in her home; he was too male, too challenging. When Camilla had suggested a male nanny, she had envisaged a quiet, much younger man; a man who somehow or other would come across as asexual and unthreatening. In fact, the very last thing she had envisaged was this man, and the more she studied him, the more astounding she found it that he should want to work for her, looking after Michael.

As she opened the door for him, impulse made her ask quickly, 'Are you sure you want this job? It can be very lonely. The others found that...and Michael isn't always as lovable as he was today.'

The hair at the back of Garrick's neck rose warningly. She was having second thoughts. He had felt it in the kitchen, sensed it when she backed off from him so surprisingly.

Quickly he reassured her. 'I'm sure. I like kids. Michael and I will get along fine . . . and besides,' he added, with what he hoped passed for sincerity, 'I need the money.'

The car parked outside her small front garden belied that fact. It was an expensive and almost brand-new Ferrari. Kate stared at it in amazement, and Garrick cursed inwardly.

He had forgotten about that, and he could hardly disclaim ownership. If he did, she might even ring the police in order to trace the owner, and then the fat would be in the fire.

'I suppose you bought it while you were working abroad,' Kate said weakly, unwittingly offering him an escape route.

'Yes. That's right,' he agreed with studied nonchalance. 'Of course, it's much older than it looks. It had to be re-registered when I came home. It's surprising what a difference new number-plates make to an old car.'

Kate didn't know all that much about cars, and so she simply accepted what he was saying, although she did inwardly question the wisdom of a man who was apparently in dire financial straits running a car that must surely be heavy on petrol. It was not her concern, she reminded herself. She was employing Rick as a nanny for Michael and nothing more.

She didn't wait to see him drive off, for which Garrick was profoundly thankful. His carphone was bleeping frantically as he unlocked the door, and he spoke into it harshly, answering its imperative summons.

He was going to have one hell of a lot of work to do if he was going to start his new 'job' by Monday morning, and he might as well get started right away.

He finished the call which was from a casual acquaintance inviting him to a 'charity' ball. No doubt hoping for a generous donation from him as a result, he reflected as he gave a cool refusal. He was generous when it came to supporting his chosen charities, but he had no time for the antics of those people who spent almost a hundred thousand pounds in order to make a couple of thousand pounds profit for a specific cause, then thought they were being generous.

He picked up the phone and punched out a number. His secretary answered, and Garrick gave him several curt instructions.

Gerald Oswald was used to Garrick's terse commands, and to being on call virtually twenty-four hours a day, but the perks of being Garrick Evans' personal assistant far more than outweighed the disadvantages.

As he drove into the private car parking bay attached to the prestigious block that housed his apartment, Garrick was surprised to discover how tired he felt.

His shirt was still slightly damp, and it smelled of baby powder, he recognised in mild disgust as he climbed out of the Ferrari and locked it.

She had smelled of it too, only on her... He frowned, disliking the turn his thoughts were taking and irritated that he should find Kate Oakley even

mildly attractive. She wasn't his type. He disliked
career women as lovers. When he was involved with
a woman, he liked her to be able to fit in with his
career demands, not to expect him to fit in with hers.
His mouth quirked a little in wryly humorous
acknowledgement of his own foibles. He doubted very
much that Kate Oakley would be quite as indulgent.

Most mornings she got up at six-thirty, she had told
him, adding coolly that he needn't follow suit.

'I enjoy the hour or so I have alone with Michael
in the morning,' she had warned him in that controlled voice she had.

Well, at that hour of the morning she was welcome
to it. He only hoped it wouldn't be too long before
Gerald was able to find him a reliable nanny who
could take over his supposed duties from him.

A little to his surprise, he discovered that he was
almost looking forward to the challenge of the coming
weeks. Of course, there could be no doubt as to the
eventual outcome. He would win, and he had no
compunction at all about what he planned to do. Fond
though she seemed to be of him—surprisingly so, in
fact—there was no doubt that it was going to be a
struggle for her to bring up the child alone. A struggle
from which he was going to free her. One day she
would be grateful to him . . . and if she wasn't . . .

His mouth compressed. The feelings of Kate Oakley
were no concern of his. No concern at all.

CHAPTER FOUR

KATE sighed and replaced the receiver. She had rung Camilla several times to tell her the news about Rick, and also to have her small but unnerving doubts as to the wisdom of what she was doing allayed by her friend's sensible counsel, but every time she dialled Camilla's number the only response she could get was a recorded message to say that Camilla and her husband had been called away indefinitely.

She was sitting in her favourite cross-legged position on the floor of Michael's room, while he crawled energetically around her, picking up building blocks. She was wearing a pair of well-washed jeans and a comfortable top. Since Michael's advent into her life, her weekends had changed dramatically: meals out, visits to the theatre and a variety of gallery and exhibition openings that had previously been a feature of her weekends had now given way to walks in the park, shopping, and if she was lucky half an hour of peace and relaxation on Sunday evening after Michael had gone to sleep and before she started going through her diary for the coming week.

Today it was too wet to spend too much time outside. In the park the leaves had lain in damp clusters on the paths, and it seemed to Kate that the temperature had dropped several degrees almost overnight.

Michael demanded her attention by dropping one of the bricks in her lap. They were brightly coloured wooden blocks that linked together to spell his name, an impulse purchase she hadn't been able to resist, and now she obligingly took the letter from him and painstakingly collected the others. As she linked them together, she was acutely conscious of an unfamiliar tension tautening her muscles, a straining awareness of the fact that she was not really concentrating on what she was doing but listening for the sound of a car outside, footsteps on the path, the ring of the doorbell. All of which could herald the arrival of Rick Evans.

Had she done the right thing? To virtually hand Michael into the care of a stranger... The girls she had previously employed had also been strangers. But that had been different; Rick was a man...

She wriggled uncomfortably, all too aware of the fact that she was being guilty of mental sexual discrimination; something she bitterly resented when it operated against her own sex. There was no reason at all why a man should not be able to take perfectly good care of a small child, and Michael had taken to Rick with an immediacy he had not exhibited towards his other nannies.

No. If she got to the heart of things, her doubts and fears were not just fuelled by concern for Michael, but by her own ambivalent feelings towards Rick Evans.

For one thing, he was so different from what she had imagined. So much more intensely male, carrying about him an aura of power she was familiar with in the heads of large corporations and other successful businessmen, but which she had not expected to find surrounding a male nanny. Because society might consider the task of looking after a child to male nanny. Because society might consider the task of looking after a child to be less meaningful than running a company?

She wriggled again, uncomfortable with her own thoughts and what she recognised as her childhood prejudices and conditioning. Until the importance of the work women did in bringing up children was not just recognised but also respected, there could be no true equality for her sex. Kate knew that, but she also knew that she herself was helping to maintain that lack of equality by her own feeling of ill-ease at the thought of employing a man to take care of Michael.

Halfway through the evening, when Rick Evans had still not returned, Kate decided that he had changed his mind. She was surprised to discover that it wasn't just relief she felt; there was also an odd sense of having won a reprieve. But a reprieve from what? Now she would be put to the trouble of starting her search all over again.

Upstairs, Michael was asleep. Kate had just been going through her diary, checking on her appointments. She already had several small clients, but she desperately needed the security that having a client like James Cameron would give her.

She got out all her meticulously filed data and started checking on it to make sure there was nothing she had missed. The two girls who worked for her had been responsible for putting together the lists of the various local TV and radio stations with the best advertising records. She herself had checked rigorously to discover which packaging companies were most likely to supply the right kind of image for the new look supermarkets, and which magazines it would be best to advertise in. She had also prepared data on which advertising agencies held the best record of success for their campaigns in the same kind of field, and, even though she knew she had already done everything it was possible to do to ensure that she won the contract, she was still unable to put her work away.

A burst of nervous energy was driving her on, a relentless feeling that there was still something she had left to do. She wasn't happy about the thought of working closely with James, she acknowledged, putting down her pen. He made her feel wary and on edge, especially when he paid her sexually loaded compliments.

She had made it clear to him firmly and pleasantly that she was not in the market for a sexual relationship, and he had appeared to accept this with good grace, but something niggled at her: an inner awareness that he was not going to be an easy man to deal with. But she needed the contract.

She was so busy worrying about it that she almost missed the sound her nerves had been stretched tensely to catch all day. It was only the sharp slam of a car door that broke through her concentration, making her half rise from her chair, so that she was on her feet when the front door bell rang.

She went to open it.

'Sorry I'm late,' Garrick apologised tersely. 'My stuff's in the car. Is it all right if I bring it in?'

Gerald, excellent assistant that he was, had managed to keep his face wooden and composed when he had explained to him that for the next few weeks he was going to be virtually incommunicado, and that all his appointments would have to be cancelled.

He had not even said anything when Garrick had added that he was going to need a computer terminal that would allow him to tap into the complex system set up in their main office, and that the only way he, Gerald, would have of reaching him would be either via this terminal or on the carphone, and then only between a certain set of hours.

It was only when Garrick had instructed him to find him a discreet and properly trained nanny to take charge of a nine-month-old child that he had shown any reaction, and even then he had controlled it quickly.

Garrick had had no difficulty in realising that his assistant thought that the child in question was his own, and he had not enlightened him. Time enough for that later, once he had sole guardianship of the boy.

The Ferrari was parked outside; Kate could see the scarlet gleam of its paintwork in the streetlights. Garrick had to make several trips between it and his new quarters. Kate left him to it, not wanting to appear curious about his personal possessions. She stifled a yawn as she tidied up her papers.

She was tired and looking forward to an early night. She heard the car door slam and then the front door close. Garrick knocked briefly on the sitting-room door and then opened it.

'All done. I expect you'll want to run through Michael's routine again with me.' He pushed back the cuff of the same blouson jacket he had worn the previous day. 'Can you give me, say, half an hour to get my stuff unpacked, and then we can discuss it?'

Too startled by his assumption of command to object, Kate could only stare at the closing door. When he came back, she deliberately wouldn't offer him a cup of coffee or a drink. One thing she intended to make very clear to her new employee was that he was exactly that, and that she was the one who gave the commands, although she doubted that she had the flair to deliver them with quite the high-handed insouciance he had just employed.

When he came back downstairs, she was ready for him. As he knocked and walked into the sitting-room, she stood up and handed him a printed list.

'I think this makes everything clear,' she told him calmly. 'I've got an early start tomorrow, so I'm going to bed now. If you want any supper, please help yourself. I think you'll find everything you need in the kitchen.'

With a cool nod of dismissal, she opened the door and went straight upstairs.

Garrick stared after her, frowning, conscious of an odd let-down feeling, which he decided was all too probably caused by the pangs of hunger attacking his stomach.

The last time he had eaten had been lunch time, having been too busy to make the dinner date with friends he had previously arranged. But the thought of making himself something to eat was totally unappealing, as was the notion of going to bed at half-past ten at night.

He wasn't quite sure what Kate Oakley was trying to prove by her actions, but if she thought she was in some way asserting her authority over him by sending him supperless to bed, like a naughty child . . . Grimly he opened the door, having picked up the set of keys Kate had given him.

She heard the powerful roar of the car as she stepped out of the bath. She walked into her bedroom just in time to see the lights of the Ferrari as it disappeared out of sight. Where was he going?

It was no concern of hers, she told herself sharply. Just as long as he took proper care of Michael, what he chose to do in his own time was his own affair.

Affair perhaps being the operative word. He didn't look like the kind of man who lived the life of a celibate. She wondered who she was, the woman who shared his bed, and was horrified by the immediacy of the images that flashed through her mind.

From where had she got this ability to visualise so precisely the structured grace of his naked body? From what dark corners of her psyche came this unwanted awareness of him as a man? Wherever it came from, it would have to be banished.

Tired as she was, she couldn't sleep; at least not until she heard the Ferrari return, and the comforting click of the front door as Rick locked it behind him. He was back. She fell asleep before she could question just why knowing that had been important enough to keep her awake.

Garrick had been out for a meal which now sat uncomfortably heavily on his stomach. It was gone midnight when he got back, and it took him almost a further two hours to set up the terminal to his satisfaction.

As a consequence he slept through Kate's half-past six alarm, and his first intimation that a new way of life had started came when Kate rapped sharply on his door, having returned from her walk with Michael.

'I'm going to give Michael his breakfast now,' she announced, half opening the door but not walking into the room. 'And then I'll be leaving for the office shortly afterwards. I'll put him in his playpen when I've fed him.'

A judicious move, she had discovered in her early days of looking after him, since it gave her time to get changed into her office clothes without any danger of Michael's sticky fingers coming into contact with them.

Kate was a meticulous timekeeper and worked to a very strict routine. At eight o'clock, she walked into Michael's nursery to kiss him goodbye, as she did every morning. There was as yet no sign of Rick, although she could hear sounds of movement from his room. She called out a brief 'goodbye' to him, as she went downstairs to collect her briefcase.

She arrived at her office at ten to nine and unlocked the door. Soon after, Sara and Harriet, the two girls who worked for her, arrived within minutes of one another. While Harriet made them all a mug of coffee, Kate opened the mail.

It was disappointingly bereft of new business. Times were hard in the city; the euphoria caused by the 'Big Bang' change in the stock-market had died away to be replaced by a new atmosphere of caution. People were not prepared to risk their reputation with a PR agent who was not known to them, and the clients Kate did have were in the main small, struggling businesses like her own.

Camilla had helped as much as she could, and Kate had got some business via that help. If she could just succeed with James...

She dialled Camilla's office number and learned from her husband's secretary that his father had had a heart attack over the weekend and that, although he had returned home, Camilla was staying in the country to help her mother-in-law and would not be returning for some time.

Thanking her for the information, Kate replaced the receiver. She was still uneasy in her mind about the wisdom of employing Rick, but what other option did she have? The agency she had used previously had pointed out rather sharply to her when she rang them that the turnover of nannies in her household was alarmingly high. Their tone had implied that the fault lay not with their girls but with Kate herself, and perhaps it did, she acknowledged. Perhaps she expected too much of people, set standards that were too high; then again, perhaps in other households there were others to share the responsibility of the caring: partners, parents, family. She had no one.

The words seemed to echo dully inside her head, tormenting her, and yet previously she had congratulated herself on her solitary state because it left her free of any emotional ties so that she could pursue her career without any interruptions.

But that had been before Michael...and now, ironically, despite the havoc he had caused in her life, she knew that she could not bear to part with him.

Before, she had never understood what drove some single women to have a child, especially when they had demanding careers to cope with. She had always assumed that she was lacking in that maternal instinct, but now she was not so sure. Over recent weeks, she had sometimes realised to her horror that Michael had crept into her thoughts when they ought to have been concentrated exclusively on her work. She had even caught herself staring dreamily into space, remembering how he had smiled at her, or some new clever skill he had learned.

Outside in the main office she could hear the two girls talking about their weekends. Harriet had been home to the Cotswolds to stay with her parents. Sara had spent her free time with her fiancé who was on leave from the army. Both girls came from moneyed families and worked for her for a very small salary indeed. They were both Camilla's god-daughters and, fortunately, despite their cushioned backgrounds, hard workers. Kate had never felt the remotest twinge of envy of them, but suddenly, listening to them, she was bleakly conscious of how empty of people her life was. What would happen to Michael if anything befell her?

She could feel an unfamiliar sensation of panic claiming her, swelling and building inside her, a terrifying awareness of Michael's vulnerability. Apart from her, he had no one.

Her phone rang and she picked it up.

'Ah, Kate...how are you this morning?'

'James . . . I'm fine, and you?'

'Look, I was wondering if I could bring our dinner date forward to Wednesday. I'm going to be rather tied up later in the week—a possible new acquisition.'

Kate's heart sank. She was as sure as she could be that her presentation was good, but she had wanted to discuss it with Camilla before submitting it to him. What was it about having a dependent child to look after that was so damaging to a woman's self-confidence? Perhaps it had something to do with the sleepless nights, she decided grimly, as she acceded to James's request.

'I'll pick you up, shall I? Say eight o'clock . . .'

Kate thanked him and gave him her address, making a mental note to be ready on time so that she didn't have to invite him in. It would do nothing for the image she was so determined to cultivate for James to discover Michael . . . or his nanny.

Unless she was lunching with clients, Kate did not have an official lunch hour. It was just gone one when her phone rang. Both girls were out and she picked it up, giving her name absently.

'Michael won't eat his dinner.'

The abrupt comment delivered in an exceedingly irate male voice startled her for a second.

'Kate, are you there?'

Kate? When had she given him permission to use her Christian name? The girls she had employed had all referred to her very correctly as Miss Oakley.

'Yes. Yes, I am here,' she responded crisply. 'What did you give him to eat?'

He told her and she frowned a little, realising he had used one of her emergency standby tins of pre-

pared food, instead of using fresh ingredients and
blending them as she preferred.

'That isn't one he likes very much,' she told him.
'Try the banana pudding, he seems to have a weakness
for that.'

'Thanks.'

'Oh, and Rick...'

She could almost hear his impatience humming
down the telephone wires.

'Yes?' he responded tersely.

'In future, perhaps you would follow my instructions and prepare Michael's food from fresh ingredients, using the blender. I think I did mention to you
that I don't like him having convenience meals unless
it's absolutely necessary.'

As he replaced the receiver, she thought she heard
him mutter, 'It was necessary, believe me,' but the
mutter had not been clear enough to be sure.

Her fears for Michael in her own absence, always
latent, no matter who was in charge of him, rose to
swamp her with guilt, distracting her from concentrating on the presentation she was trying to prepare.

What on earth had she done, allowing a mere man
to take charge of Michael? A man who, it seemed,
had flagrantly flouted her instructions and fed him
tinned baby food. A man who didn't have the sense
to read her instructions properly, who rang her up at
work and completely destroyed her concentration.

What she needed right now, she recognised was
some calming reassurance; the kind of reassurance
that Camilla invariably gave her, but Camilla had
problems of her own.

*   *   *

The afternoon brought a flurry of telephone calls, and the promise of some additional business from one of her existing clients who was thinking of expanding. In order to make up for the time she had lost worrying about Michael, Kate had to work late. Normally she enjoyed the peace of the office when she had it to herself, but this evening she found it hard to concentrate.

At half-past seven she gave in and called it a day. It took her over an hour to get home due to a problem with the underground, and when she did she was cold and tired.

As she put her key in the lock and opened the door, the house seemed unnaturally silent. Her heart did a somersault, all manner of terrible images flooding her brain. Something had happened to Michael . . . an accident. Dropping her briefcase, she rushed upstairs. Michael was standing up in his playpen, holding on to the bars. He grinned when he saw her. His rompers were filthy and his bib was generously stained with what looked like tomato purée. The room looked as though a whirlwind had hit it, toys strewn everywhere, and there in the middle of the chaos, dead to the world in the Victorian nursing chair she had bought and re-covered herself, lay Rick Evans—fast asleep.

Kate studied him covertly, noting the way the thick, dark lashes gave him an air of vulnerability. He was wearing jeans, and his shirt, like Michael's rompers, looked decidedly worse for wear.

As he crowed his delight at seeing her, Michael held up his arms to her and promptly sat down on his well-padded bottom. Kate picked him up, frowning as she discovered the odd shapelessness of his nappy. A brief investigation showed her that, whatever else Rick Evans might know about small children, he was not apparently *au fait* with the art of fastening a nappy.

She redid his handiwork to her own and Michael's satisfaction, and then quietly set about restoring order to the untidy nursery while Michael chattered unintelligibly to her, telling her all about his day.

He was a good-natured baby, physically affectionate and responsive, and Kate had been surprised to discover how much she enjoyed holding and cuddling his small body.

The room tidy, she picked him up, enjoying the way he nestled against her, before remembering that she was still wearing her office clothes. Normally the first thing she did when she got in was get changed. Thanks to Rick Evans her routine had been overset, and the result was that Michael was happily chewing on the shoulder of her very expensive Paul Costello suit.

Taking him with her, she went through to her own room, putting Michael down on the floor.

Stripping off her suit and blouse, she was standing in her satin teddy, reaching into her wardrobe for a pair of jeans, when her bedroom door was suddenly thrust open and Rick Evans walked in, calling anxiously, 'Michael? Oh . . . I didn't realise you were back.'

'Obviously not,' Kate agreed drily.

She wasn't used to men walking into her bedroom, and even though common sense told her that she was as decorously clad as any woman lying on a summer beach, she felt acutely vulnerable and uncomfortable with him standing there, watching her.

'I must have fallen asleep. I had no idea it was so late.' He yawned as he spoke, stretching so that his shirt clung tautly to his body.

'Yes,' Kate agreed tersely. She was holding her jeans in front of her as though they afforded some form of protection. But against what? He seemed to have no idea that she found his presence in her bedroom both an intrusion and embarrassment, and to her astonishment, instead of apologising and leaving, he sat down on her bed, picking Michael up and making the little boy laugh as he tossed him into the air and caught him again.

'Perhaps you'd like to take Michael and get him ready for his bath,' she suggested in some exasperation when he made no move to leave.

He looked at her over the little boy's head, and Kate was suddenly acutely aware of the way in which the satin fabric clung to her body. She moved her weight uncomfortably from one foot to the other.

'Aren't we going to have dinner first?'

Dinner? Kate forgot her embarrassment and frowned.

'I shall be having a light supper when I feel hungry,' she told him freezingly. 'If you had read my instructions you would have realised that you should have had *your* meal at six o'clock, after Michael had had his tea. Look, I don't think this is going to work,' Kate told him, suddenly exasperated. 'I'm sure you're every bit as good as your agency says, but I don't think for a child as young as Michael...'

'Michael ate the instructions,' he interrupted her. 'Well, at least—I left them on the table and he got hold of them, but by the time I'd realised what had happened it was too late.'

Kate could visualise the scene all too easily. Michael had a propensity for destruction, unlike anything she had previously experienced.

'Please give me another chance . . . I need this job.'

The very fact that he obviously found it very difficult to ask her softened her reluctance to keep him on. Who knew what kind of personal problems he might have which she knew nothing about? If she was honest with herself, it was his maleness and not his mistakes that was upsetting her so much. And that, surely, was her problem and not his?

'I'll give you another copy of the instructions,' she told him quietly, 'and tonight, as it's so late . . . I was only going to have quiche and salad for supper, but you're welcome to share it.'

What on earth was she saying? He looked as surprised as she felt, and she made a hurried attempt to re-establish the right amount of distance between them by saying coolly, 'In future, please don't come into my bedroom. To be honest with you, I find it rather strange that you did, especially in view of your complaints about your last employer.'

He looked almost mystified and she reminded him curtly, 'I was told that your last employer made unwanted advances towards you.'

'Er—yes . . . but you see, I thought you were out. I woke up and found that Michael had gone and I was in such a panic . . .'

Kate knew that feeling all too well.

'Yes, it's surprising how far they can travel,' she agreed wryly.

Garrick turned his head and looked at her. Nothing in the day had gone as he had planned. For a start, he had not been able to get hold of a nanny, and, although he had witnessed his mother caring for countless numbers of small children over the years, he had soon discovered that watching someone else do the work was one thing, doing it oneself was quite another.

It had taken him nearly an hour just to change Michael's nappy. For one thing the little boy just wouldn't keep still, and for another he couldn't seem to get the damn thing secure. Then there had been the débâcle of lunch—a meal which he had not been able to consume himself, since by the time he managed to get some of the revolting puréed mixture into Michael and clean up the mess this operation had involved, he had totally lost his appetite.

Gerald, summoned to drive round to the house with a large flask of coffee and some sandwiches at four o'clock in the afternoon, had taken one look at his normally immaculate boss and simply stared at him open-mouthed.

'You breathe one word of this to anyone and you're fired,' Garrick had told him threateningly.

They had gone through the mail together, while Michael played on the floor. Gerald had left promising to do everything he could to expedite the arrival of a properly trained nanny.

'The problem is,' he explained earnestly to Garrick, 'that none of the reputable agencies are keen on allowing one of their girls to work for an unknown man. Well, you can see their point, but you said not to disclose your name . . .'

'Couldn't you give them yours?' Garrick had demanded testily.

'Well, yes, but you see they wanted to see the house and the baby. It seems that good nannies are in very great demand.'

'I can see why,' Garrick had told him grimly.

After Gerald left it had been time to give Michael his tea. His first attempt to use the blender had resulted in the fiasco which even at this minute still decorated the kitchen, despite his attempts to remove most of the evidence.

It had been after that he had fallen asleep. Now he felt more tired than he had ever done in his life, and that included cross-Atlantic travel and the resultant jet lag.

He was also extremely hungry. So hungry that even quiche and salad made his mouth water.

As he carried Michael back to his bedroom, he wondered where on earth the day had gone. He had nearly had heart failure when he woke up and found the little boy gone, and in the ten seconds it had taken him to find out, he had wondered what on earth he was going to tell Kate when she demanded an explanation for the baby's absence.

It only struck him as he put Michael down in his playpen how odd it was that his first concern had been for how he was going to tell Kate, rather than the upset Michael's potential disappearance might cause to his own plans.

He frowned heavily. His whole purpose in carrying out this idiotic charade was to collect enough proof to ensure that the legal system would give him sole custody of Michael through the negligence of his present guardian. And yet in his own heart of hearts he knew already that Kate Oakley was devoted to the little boy, and that she would defend and protect him as aggressively as a tigress with her cub.

Kate's feelings for Michael were not his concern, he reminded himself. If she wanted a child so desperately, there was nothing to stop her finding a man and having one of her own. She was an attractive woman, with a surprisingly voluptuous body. Very few men would turn down the opportunity to make love with a woman like her. She could have as many children as she wished.

He resolutely ignored the inner voice that pointed out austerely that so could he. It was different for a man: a man would always be vulnerable to the woman who carried his child. No matter what agreement might have been reached, women were notoriously emotionally unbalanced. He wanted the child without the complications of the mother. He wanted Michael.

Dressed in jeans and a sweater, Kate went through to Michael's bedroom, stopping on the threshold when she saw that Michael was in his playpen while his nanny was standing staring out of the window.

'Perhaps you'd like to go and get changed?' she suggested as he carried the plastic bath into the shower room. She deftly undressed Michael as she waited for the bath to fill. 'Oh, and remind me to show you how to fasten a nappy,' she added drily when Rick turned round to watch her.

She was surprised to see a faint burn of colour darkening his skin.

'All right, I admit it,' he agreed harshly. 'I don't have very much experience with such young children. But I do need this job... more than you can possibly realise, and I give you my word that while Michael's in my care, I'll see to it that he doesn't come to any kind of harm.'

Strangely she found his admission and his promise far more reassuring than she found his original contention that he was fully capable of looking after the small boy. Just for a moment she had seen something human and real in his eyes, something that touched a chord inside her.

She was tired of constantly worrying about the skill and responsibility of whoever was in charge of Michael. She trusted this man at least to display common sense and hard-headedness, even if he might lack a few of the more practical mothering skills. And who knew, perhaps Camilla was right when she said it was never too soon for a child to experience the male as well as the female influence in its life.

For better or worse, Rick Evans was Michael's nanny. For better or worse... odd that she should have picked those words from out of the marriage ceremony.

'Perhaps you'd like to bath Michael?' she said briskly to cover the confusion of her feelings. 'I'll stand and watch.'

'I think that might be a good idea,' Garrick agreed. 'Oh, and by the way, I had a small problem with the blender.'

CHAPTER FIVE

Who other than the male of the species would dream of filling a blender with hard-boiled eggs and heaven alone knew what else, and then switch it on without the top on? Kate reflected wearily when she had removed the last of the mess from her normally pristine kitchen walls.

It was gone eleven o'clock and she hadn't done a single stroke of office work. What had happened to that interlude of calm quietude she normally enjoyed after her evening meal?

Rick had retired to his room to tamper with his computer, after she had refused his solicitous offer to help with the washing up.

'I have a machine,' she had pointed out drily to him. She was so tired now that her bones ached, but she could hardly leave the mess in the kitchen to be tackled by Mrs Riley who came in once a week to clean for her.

There, at last it was done. What she needed now was a hot, milky drink and an even hotter bath, and then bed. At least the activity of the evening had kept her from worrying about the fact that she hadn't been able to test her presentation out on Camilla.

Rick Evans came into the kitchen just as she was pouring milk into a pan.

'Supper?' he asked her, looking pleased at the prospect.

'No, *not* supper,' she told him coldly. 'Simply a hot drink which I am making for *myself*. *I* don't eat supper, but if you wish to do so, please feel free to make yourself something. Actually, Michael's previous nannies normally preferred to take advantage of the fact that I'm here in the evening to take a few hours off.'

'Meaning that's what you'd prefer me to do?' Garrick asked her shrewdly.

Something in the way he looked at her made Kate feel almost uncomfortable, and she found herself saying hastily, 'No...no, not at all,' which was exactly the opposite of what she meant.

'Do you go out much yourself in the evenings?' he asked her carelessly as he walked behind her to open the fridge door and inspect the contents.

It was a natural enough question, but Kate found she was stiffening slightly, ready to bristle with defensiveness should he indicate either by a look or a comment that he found it odd that a young woman of her age preferred to concentrate on her career rather than go out on dates.

'Sometimes—on business,' she told him coolly, letting her voice indicate that she was not pleased that he should question her on her personal life.

He didn't take the hint, removing a carton of eggs from the fridge, saying approvingly, 'Free range...good. I think I'll make myself an omelette, if that's OK with you,' and then adding before she could say a word, 'So when do you get the chance to let your hair down—meet men?'

Kate turned on him angrily. 'My private life isn't your concern,' she began, her eyes widening in startled shock as he put down the carton of eggs and took hold of her, virtually lifting her off her feet.

As she started to protest, her eyes registering her shock that he should manhandle her in such a way, he put her down, and deftly removed the pan of boiling milk from the hot-plate behind her.

'Sorry about that, but it was going to boil over,' he said easily, leaving her scarlet with mortification and temper.

She was beginning to bitterly regret her soft-headedness in allowing him to stay. It was becoming quite plain to her that he did not have the slightest idea of how a nanny should behave. It was not that Kate expected her employees to be subservient toward her—far from it. But she did expect a quite natural acknowledgement of the fact that their relationship was one in which hers was the more dominant role. Rick Evans seemed to have absolutely no awareness of this fact, and looking at him, standing in her small kitchen, watching her with eyes that held intelligent awareness of her confusion, and something else that was less obvious and harder to define, she found it very hard indeed to believe that this was a man who had been so intimidated by the sexual overtures of his previous employer that he had sought another job.

For all that she had known him only a very short time indeed, she found it hard to imagine that anyone, male or female, might intimidate him.

She reached for the pan of milk, pouring it shakily into her mug.

'I'm going to bed now,' she told him, trying to sound both cool and in control. 'And if you must use the blender, please remember to put the lid on.'

Garrick watched her go. Her back was ramrod stiff, but her eyes had given her away when he touched her. He had seen all too clearly that flash of near panic darken her eyes. Women did not normally panic when he touched them. Far from it. She obviously wasn't used to being touched, either. So she couldn't be involved in a relationship. That was a pity. A woman in love might quite easily tend to neglect the small child in her care in favour of that lover, and he was beginning to suspect that he would need all the ammunition he could find if he was going to succeed in his intention of taking the child away from her. No judge seeing them together could fail to see the relationship which she had already established with Michael.

What he needed now was a thoroughly reliable young woman he could employ as Michael's nanny. Someone who could take charge of him and establish a relationship with him that would eventually oust Kate from his affections. But what woman of that calibre would ever agree to the deception that would be needed for her to be able to work with Michael without Kate's knowledge? And how would he be able to trust a woman who did?

As he ate his omelette, he reflected rather wryly that this evening he should have been attending the premiere of a new film, with supper afterwards at the Ritz. His date for the evening had not been at all pleased at the cancellation of their arrangements, so Gerald had told him.

It struck him as he finished his meal that things weren't going according to plan. It had been a long time since anything had been allowed to disrupt the smooth running of his life, and even longer since that 'anything' had been a woman.

The problem was that he had not taken into account the effect of the enforced intimacy of living in such close contact with another adult human being, especially an adult female human being.

Kate had her hot bath and fell asleep the moment her head touched the pillow. When Michael cried out, she was awake instantly, groping in the dark for the switch to her bedside-light, pulling on her robe even as she registered the fact that it was three o'clock in the morning.

With the central heating off, her bedroom felt chilly and she shivered as she made her way to Michael's room. As she had suspected the moment his cry had woken her, there was no sign of Rick Evans.

Picking Michael up out of his cot, she checked automatically that he was not running a temperature and that there was nothing else obviously wrong with him. He was wet, which she had half expected, and now that he had his favourite adult with him, he was quite happy to stop crying and nuzzle contentedly into her shoulder. Sitting down in the nursing chair with him, Kate studied him severely.

'There's nothing wrong with you at all, is there?' she chided him softly.

He gurgled and grinned, reaching out to tug on her hair.

'You're a fraud, that's what you are,' Kate told him. 'Waking me up in the middle of the night just so that you can have a cuddle.'

Her expression belied the severity of her words, and Kate herself was still half surprised by the tender responsiveness that Michael always managed to arouse within her. By rights she ought to be thoroughly cross at being woken out of her badly needed sleep, but the pleasure of cuddling the soft, warm body . . . the way Michael smiled and gurgled at her, more than made up for her initial irritation.

Engrossed in the little boy, it was a shock to hear Rick Evans saying softly from the open doorway, 'And who can blame him?'

Instantly Kate was acutely conscious of her untidy hair and shabby dressing-gown. All her life she had fought against appearing vulnerable to others, and now here was this man, a stranger, an employee from whom she ought to have been able to preserve a protective distance, and yet who made her feel acutely conscious of herself and him in a way that made her feel acutely uncomfortable.

For instance, now as he watched her with Michael, she was intensely aware of the drag of her cotton nightdress against her breasts; sensitive to the sensation of the fabric in a way she had never known before.

She was equally conscious of the fact that Rick Evans was wearing a towelling robe beneath the hem of which his legs were bare, suggesting that he had pulled it on to cover his nakedness.

A soft shiver gripped her, convulsing her body on a hot tide of shame. It was both ridiculous and foolish for her to be so aware of him as a man. It suggested a weakness, a vulnerability she had not hitherto realised she possessed.

Anxiety coiled tensely in her stomach, locking her body into rigid watchfulness. She didn't like the way Rick Evans made her feel, she didn't like her unwanted awareness of him as a man, and she liked even less her body's awareness of itself as acutely female. She wasn't used to this kind of experience. The male sex was a race she had determinedly held at a distance, permitting no intimate place in her life.

It had been desperation which had prompted her to agree to Camilla's suggestion that she hire a male nanny, and a ridiculous and dangerous compassion which had led her into allowing Rick Evans to stay, despite his obvious lack of experience with very young children. She had not given enough thought to the problems that the intimacy of sharing such a small house was bound to cause.

Why not? Normally she was careful and cautious in all that she did, never allowing herself to make a decision until she had explored all the possible results.

She had already given herself the answer. Sheer desperation, plus the anxiety of carrying the sole responsibility of both Michael and the business. Since Michael had come into her life, she had lost some of her armour of confidence. The little boy's vulnerability had transferred itself to her. She no longer only had herself to worry about; she had a small dependent child as well. And, just as Michael had shown her an unexpected vein of love and need within herself, so he had shown her a corresponding vulnerability and uncertainty. She was no longer the cool, controlled woman who believed herself to be invulnerable.

And Camilla had deceived her, she thought bitterly. Oh, not deliberately. No, she was quite sure that her friend had not meant to give her a totally erroneous impression of the kind of man Rick Evans would be. She knew her better than that. No. Her friend had acted in all good faith. It was not her fault that Kate had expected to have to deal with quite a mild-mannered type of man . . . the type of man who instinctively shied away from the female sex, the type of man one would quite naturally expect to meet on learning of his inability to cope with the sexual advances of a forceful female employer. Instead she had been confronted by a man who seemed the exact opposite of what she had expected.

Michael had gone to sleep. He lay heavily against her. Lost in thought, she wasn't even aware of Rick crossing the room until he gently lifted the sleeping baby from her arms. Her body tensed as his hand brushed accidently against the soft curve of her breast, her face unwittingly betraying her shock.

Garrick saw it and recognised her shock for what it was. The women he knew were sexually experienced and sophisticated. The accidental touch of a man's hand against their body did not cause them to go pale and then flush, their eyes mirroring open bewilderment at the recognition of their awareness of him as a man.

It made him feel both angry and protective at the same time. He didn't want to be aware of Kate's sexual vulnerability. It gave him an unfair advantage over her in this battle she didn't even know had begun.

He frowned as he carried Michael over to his cot, wondering why he should find the idea of taking advantage of her vulnerability so distasteful.

Garrick wasn't used to vulnerable women. The women he knew, knew exactly what life was all about. They would never allow themselves to be woken up in the middle of the night by the cry of a child who wasn't theirs.

Kate focused blindly on his robe-clad back, trying to will away the memory of the fluttering sensation of unfamiliar pleasure she had felt when he touched her. It was so very shaming, that flutter of pleasure; so embarrassingly unwanted and unlooked for, and that knowledge made her clench her muscles painfully and say curtly to Rick Evans, 'It might be a good idea if you invested in a pair of pyjamas. I'm beginning to understand why your previous employer might have thought her advances would be reciprocated.'

'Is that how you see me?' Garrick countered smoothly. 'As sexually available?'

He was on familiar ground now, his expression tinged with faint amusement as he turned from the cot to look at her.

To Kate, his amusement, coming on top of the confusion of her own awareness of his effect on her senses, was like acid thrown on to her skin. She burned with the torment of realising what he thought, immediately getting to her feet and drawing her shabby robe protectively round her body.

'I see you as a nanny who has so far shown an appalling lack of awareness of his duties and responsibility,' she said pointedly. 'In fact, I'm beginning to think——'

She was going to dismiss him, Garrick realised, cursing his own stupidity. Just because her vulner-

ability had caught him off guard, that had been no
reason for him to try to undermine her self-confidence
by underlining his awareness of the sexual tension between them.

In some perverse way, he had *wanted* her to react
sexually to him, he recognised, almost as though by
inviting her to recognise and acknowledge that faint
sexual frisson he could free himself of his own guilt
in what he was doing. And in attempting to do so he
had created a potential hazard to his own ultimate
success in proving her unfit to have charge of Michael.
If she dismissed him now, it would be ten times harder
for him to gather the information he needed.

'No, please...' he interrupted her quickly, and then,
gambling desperately on the reality of the sense of
humour he suspected she possessed, he added with a
smile, 'I promise I'll go out and buy myself a pair of
pyjamas first thing in the morning.' Shrewdly he re-
frained from pointing out that if she dismissed him
she would undoubtedly face problems in finding a
suitable replacement quickly, sensing that to challenge her would have the opposite effect from what
he wanted.

His teasing comment gave Kate time to reflect on
her own behaviour. She was over-reacting, there was
no doubt about it. If she carried on like this... It
was almost as though she were looking for an excuse
to get rid of him because she was frightened of her
own reaction to him, and that was impossible.

'And a manual on how to take care of a baby,' she
suggested wryly, acknowledging that he could stay.

Long after she had gone back to bed, Kate was still
awake. As a consequence, she overslept, waking only

when she was disturbed by someone shaking her out of her deep sleep.

She opened her eyes reluctantly and focused on Garrick in confusion.

'It's eight o'clock,' he told her. 'I thought you'd want me to wake you up. I've made you a cup of coffee.'

Gone eight? That was impossible. But a quick look at her alarm told her it wasn't! It was the first time in her working life that anything like this had happened. Panic hit her as she realised that she was going to be late.

'Michael's still asleep as well.'

'You should have woken me earlier,' Kate told him fretfully.

'I heard your alarm go off, and I presumed you'd heard it as well. Can I do anything to help?'

'No. Not really.'

The moment he left the room Kate jumped out of bed, showering quickly, and pulling on the first clothes that came to hand. There wasn't time to wind her hair into its normal immaculate chignon, and she was acutely conscious of the heavy mass of her hair as she hurried downstairs.

The rich aroma of freshly brewed coffee filled the kitchen. She was hungry, but there wasn't time for her to have anything to eat. She rushed into the sitting-room, gathered up her papers, mentally calculating how long it was going to take her to reach her office. The girls would wonder what on earth had happened to her. Luckily Sara had a spare set of keys, so they could at least let themselves in.

And it would have to be today, when she had a lot on. Three appointments with prospective clients, and a celebratory lunch she couldn't possibly get out of with a client for whom her PR work had resulted in a twenty per cent increase in business.

There was also the normal paperwork to get through, and then at six she had a cocktail party to attend at a new gallery which had just opened and where she was hoping to persuade the owners to give a 'view' for one of her new clients, an artist who specialised in very delicate and appealing watercolours.

She was just stuffing the last of her papers into her briefcase when Rick walked into the sitting-room.

'Come and have your breakfast. Grapefruit, wholemeal toast and coffee. I hope that's OK.'

Her mouth watered desperately, but she shook her head.

'Thanks, but no. I haven't got time. I'm already running late.'

'You've got ten minutes,' Rick told her inexorably. 'I've ordered you a cab and he won't be here for fifteen minutes. Ten minutes to have your breakfast. Five minutes to clean your teeth and get your coat on.'

A cab? She stared at him in confusion. She wasn't used to someone else taking charge of her life like this, and Rick took advantage of her momentary bewilderment to gently usher her into the kitchen.

Her breakfast had been set out for her on the counter: the wholemeal toast was deliciously warm, the coffee fragrant and strong, just how she liked it, and the grapefruit properly segmented and free of sugar.

'I'll just go up and check on Michael,' she heard him saying, and as he disappeared she wondered if he had guessed that she preferred to eat her breakfast alone and in silence. It was remarkable how efficiently he had taken charge.

She was just applying a fresh coat of lipstick when her taxi arrived. Rick was still upstairs with Michael, and she only realised when she was in the cab that she hadn't told him that she wouldn't be in until late. She would have to ring him from the office.

In the event, she didn't need to. Garrick rang her at four o'clock, his voice terse as he told her that Michael wasn't very well.

'What's wrong with him?' Kate demanded anxiously. 'Have you called the doctor?'

'I don't think it's that serious. He's got a temperature, and he's very fretful. Can you come home?'

Could she go home? Her heart sank. Of course she couldn't. She had a thousand things to do, and then the cocktail party, which it was essential that she attend if she was to persuade the gallery owner to take her client.

She took a deep breath and said quietly and firmly, 'No, Rick, I can't. *You* are Michael's nanny. If you think it's necessary, then you must ring the doctor. The number's on the pad by the phone. Oh, and by the way, I shan't be back until around nine. There's a gallery opening I have to attend.'

As he placed the receiver back, Garrick looked with grim satisfaction at the recorder he had placed next to it. If he had written the words for her himself, he couldn't have chosen anything more damning. A mother who refused to come home when her child needed her. How could that look in court?

He reran the tape, listening to the crisp, incisive tone of Kate's refusal as he watched Michael playing happily with his building blocks. There was nothing wrong with the little boy, and Garrick had already known that Kate would not be able to come home, not after her late start this morning, not with the schedule she had. He had looked in her diary before he woke her, and had been a little startled to see James Cameron's name there. He had had dealings with the man himself and didn't like him. He was a bully and not above asserting unwarranted pressure when he thought he could get away with it. He caught himself wondering if Kate knew about his reputation, and then dismissed the thought angrily, irritated with himself for his momentary weakness.

Kate couldn't concentrate. She put down the presentation she was working on for a potential client and tried to banish from her mind tormenting images of Michael's face. Small children were so vulnerable when they were ill. A high temperature could be nothing at all, or on the other hand...

Her imagination worked overtime, busily fuelled by her guilt. How did other women cope with these situations? she wondered miserably. Common sense told her that Rick Evans was perfectly capable of calling the doctor should the situation necessitate it, but instinct and emotion argued unremittingly that she ought to be with Michael. That it was her responsibility and duty to be with him. She pictured his flushed, uncomfortable little body, heard his plaintive cries, and before she knew what she was doing she had risen from her desk and opened the door to the outer office.

'Sara,' she asked the dark-haired girl bent over a list of local TV and radio stations, 'are you doing anything this evening?'

'I've got a date...but I could cancel it. Why?'

'I wondered if you could go to a gallery opening in my place. Michael isn't well and I have to go home.'

Pleasure and ambition brought a pink flush to her assistant's face, and in her eyes Kate read the message that she considered her foolish to miss the opportunity of making such a good contact simply because of a sick child.

Once she would have shared her view, would have gloated in the presentation of such an opportunity, without giving a thought to the child responsible for it.

'Will you be in tomorrow?' Sara asked her casually as Kate stuffed papers into her briefcase and tried to concentrate on what she was saying. Now that the decision was made, she was in a fever of impatience to get home, to see for herself how Michael was. Manlike, Rick Evans had probably not told her the worst. Feverishly she pulled on her coat, mentally picturing Michael in hospital fighting for his life...

'Tomorrow?'

Kate stared blankly at her as Sara repeated the question, her heart sinking as Sara reminded her, 'It is tomorrow that you're having dinner with James Cameron, isn't it?'

'Yes. Yes...I will be in.'

But would she? Ought she to ring James and re-arrange their meeting?

It was an evening meeting, she reminded herself. Even if she had to stay at home with Michael tomorrow, she ought to be able to make it for the meeting.

Two-fold guilt nagged at her as she managed to flag down a taxi. Breathlessly she gave him her address. So much hung on her getting James's business. By rights she ought to be concentrating on making sure that her presentation was as close to perfection as possible. She had meant to do that last night. She ought to be doing it tonight. But if Michael was ill . . .

She paid off the taxi with fingers that trembled, desperately searching in her handbag for her doorkey, for once her normal powers of organisation deserting her.

The door opened before she found her key.

'Michael? How is he? Is he worse?' she gabbled as Rick stepped back to let her in. She rushed past him, heading for Michael's bedroom.

Garrick followed her. He was still recovering from the shock of her unexpected arrival. Her white face and trembling hands had told their own story and looking at her, he had had to quell an unexpected impulse to reassure her.

Upstairs Michael was sitting in his playpen, contentedly pulling apart the complex interlocking tower Garrick had built from his locking bricks.

He beamed up at Kate when he saw her, so obviously healthy and well that Kate started to shake with relief.

'Here . . . sit down.'

She was pushed gently into a chair. She subsided into it without a word of protest, saying only, 'He's all right. There's nothing wrong with him.'

'I know,' Garrick admitted. 'I suppose I panicked. He seemed very flushed and hot, and wouldn't eat his lunch.'

Strangely enough, instead of the righteous anger she knew she ought to feel, what she did experience was an almost uncontrollable desire to burst into tears. Shock and reaction, she told herself, absently fighting to control the unfamiliar weakness.

'You should have rung me.' The words lacked conviction, sounding vague and woolly. She felt confusingly weak. 'I'd better get back to the office. I'll be late this evening.'

'A date?' Garrick questioned her, knowing it wasn't. She had gone so white that he had thought she might actually faint. He could see the struggle she was having to stop herself from betraying her emotions, and he felt a sudden surge of self-dislike.

She might not be Michael's natural mother, but there could be no doubts about her love for the little boy. Would he in the same circumstances have dropped everything to rush home to assure himself that the child was all right? He was uncomfortably aware that most probably he would not, and that while it was true that financially he was able to buy the best care there was for Michael, that care could in no way compare with Kate's love for him.

'A gallery opening,' Kate responded briefly, too drained to resent his question. 'I'd better ring the office.'

Sara was going to be very disappointed, she reflected wryly as she went downstairs and picked up the receiver. Now that she was home, she might as well get changed.

She had a couple of discreetly elegant black dresses she kept for such occasions. Neither of them were openly fashionable, but they both came from good designers and enhanced the image she wished to project.

The one she chose was plain black wool crêpe with a neat neckline and long sleeves. The neat waist and discreetly curved skirt skimmed her body rather than clinging to it. It was a business woman's dress that made a very positive statement against sexual availability.

Knowing that it was going to be a cold night, Kate wore a three-quarter-length black velvet jacket over it, that was dressy enough for an evening engagement, and plain high-heeled black shoes.

Two pearl and diamanté clips in her hair were her only concession to vanity. She was perfectly well aware that a physically attractive woman could tease and flatter a man into giving her a good deal, but that was not the way she wanted to do business, because invariably the man would expect to be given something in return.

When she went into the nursery to check on Michael, Rick Evans wasn't there. The little boy's skin felt reassuringly cool, his eyes bright and clear.

Kate kissed him and hurried downstairs, wishing she did not have this increasingly urgent desire to spend more time with him. If the rest of her sex felt like this the moment a small child arrived in their lives, then she could only marvel that so many of them were mothers as well as successful career women. Perhaps she was more anxious over Michael because he was not her own...because she felt a duty to him for Jennifer's sake which nagged at her all the time she was away from him.

Garrick watched her leave from his bedroom window. She looked tired and drawn. A mixture of guilt and irritation carried him over to the phone. He dialled the number of his own office, drumming his fingers impatiently on the the table while he waited to be connected.

'Gerald, Stephen Hesketh is opening his new gallery tonight. I need to speak to him immediately. Find out where I can get in touch with him, will you?'

'Hesketh. Didn't you buy the Canalettos through him?'

'Yes,' Garrick agreed tersely, without vouchsafing any further information.

Kate's evening went surprisingly well. Stephen Hesketh had indicated that he would be more than pleased to repay the small favour he owed her, by giving her client a private view.

Kate, who had expected to have to work very hard to persuade him to agree to her suggestion, had been caught off guard by his ready acceptance. He was not a man who was known for his good nature.

'I'll get my secretary to give you a ring to confirm it, but I think I'm free for lunch on Friday. We can discuss all the details then.'

'That's fine,' Kate told him, wondering where she could take him for a meal. To her astonishment he went on to add, 'We'll eat at the Connaught, shall we? I'll get Elise to book a table,' indicating that he was going to take her out and moreover pay the bill.

Concealing her surprise, Kate left the party early, not wanting to push her luck by staying and perhaps running the risk of him changing his mind.

Having time in hand, instead of going straight home, she rang Edmund Howarth, the artist for whom she had arranged the 'view' from a call box, giving him the good news, and then agreeing to go round and discuss the preliminary arrangements for the 'view' with him.

Edmund was a very gentle and shy man, as evidenced by his paintings. A bad stammer had isolated him as a child and he had turned to painting as an outlet for his feelings. Some of the earlier work he had shown Kate evidenced the violence of his teenage emotions, and he had once told her that he had kept them as a reminder of the depth of his despair during those younger years.

He was now in his early forties and very happily married. His wife was six years his senior and they had met when he was attending a summer school for artists. She had been teaching one of the courses, and it had been she who had first suggested that the best medium for him might not be oils but watercolours.

Kate liked both of them. She had always related better to non-threatening men.

It was gone nine when she left, conscious of the fact that she was both tired and hungry, and yet she knew from experience that once she got in her appetite would have deserted her. Tiredly she got in the taxi Edmund had called for her.

Her evening had been overwhelmingly successful, and yet it struck her as she got in the cab that there was no one with whom she could share her triumph. Camilla was still away, Michael was far too young. There was a small ache of pain inside her which she tried to dismiss. What was happening to her? Her whole focus of attention seemed to be shifting almost daily; the foundations on which she had built her life crumbling away with frightening speed; the goals she had set herself with such confidence and determination no longer anything like as clear as they had once been.

And yet now she needed to succeed more than ever. She needed to succeed to provide security for Michael and herself. She must stop spending so much of her time thinking about the little boy. She must concentrate on her work, on her career. Tiredly she closed her eyes and leaned back in the cab. Her head was starting to ache and she massaged her temple and thought longingly of a hot bath and then bed, knowing that by rights she ought to be out celebrating tonight's success with something like a champagne supper. That was, after all, the public image of a successful PR person. That was how contracts were made and contracts won. How long would it be before she was able to leave Michael in the care of others without this constant nagging sense of guilt, this fear that something would happen to him in her absence? It must be soon, otherwise she was going to tear herself apart with overwork and guilt, and that wouldn't help either of them.

Just for one treacherous second she allowed herself to wonder what it would be like to have someone to share the responsibility with her. Someone like . . . her heart thumped uncomfortably fast as a name and a face formed within her brain.

Rick Evans. It disturbed her that he should occupy so many of her thoughts. It was just overtiredness, that was all. Overtiredness and reaction to the adjustments she was having to make in taking on a male nanny. This constant and unwanted awareness of him would fade in time. After all, she had never reacted like this before, never experienced such an awareness before. It was bound to fade. It had to fade.

CHAPTER SIX

TENSELY Kate studied the presentation in front of her; she had been through it so many times before, she suspected that she was no longer objective enough to make any useful criticism of it, but nervous energy drove her on, refusing to allow her to relax and let her body recoup itself as she knew she ought.

Tonight she was having dinner with James. By the end of the week the entire future of her young company would be decided. So much hung on James's decision. She had other clients, of course, but none of them were of the financial standing of James.

With James as her client, she would automatically be moving up the status ladder; she would attract larger and wealthier clients; she would be able to expand, to allow herself to relax a little. Success in obtaining James's business meant security for Michael and herself.

She knew her presentation was good. The chain of supermarkets was only a very small part of James's empire, but he had tacitly indicated that success with the supermarkets would lead to the chosen PR company getting the rest of his business. Yes, she knew her presentation was good, but what she didn't know was the strength of her rivals' presentations.

If only Camilla was here. She needed the boost of being able to talk to someone who understood her and who understood her business, but when she had rung her home this morning, she had learned that her father-in-law had suffered a second heart attack and that Camilla was continuing to stay with her mother-in-law.

She put the presentation away carefully with a faint sigh. Given free choice, she would have preferred to discuss her suggestions either here in her own office or in James's.

The idea of having dinner alone with him in his flat did not appeal to her. She knew his reputation, but she felt reasonably sure that she had already convinced him that she was not in the market for a one-night stand or even an affair.

And it was true, as he had pointed out to her when she had originally expressed dislike of his suggested venue, that they would be able to discuss and study her presentation far more easily in the comfort of his flat than in some restaurant.

She had planned to leave the office early, but a sudden rash of telephone calls delayed her, and it was gone six when she eventually hurried breathlessly up to her front door.

By rights she ought to have taken a cab rather than use the underground, but the long years of rigorous self-denial after she had left the children's home had left their mark, and, while she wasn't mean, she was very careful about what she spent on herself.

From the sounds reaching her from upstairs, Rick was obviously giving Michael his bath. Discarding her coat and gloves in her own room, Kate hurried through to the nursery.

Rick had put the bath on the floor on a large towel rather than use its stand. Shirt sleeves rolled up, he was kneeling beside it with his back to her, both he and Michael totally engrossed in a game they were playing.

Watching them, Kate felt a sharp surge of envy. Normally his bathtime was her special time with Michael, and she resented the fact that Rick was taking that from her, even while she recognised that it would hardly be fair to the little boy to disturb his routine to fit in with her own uncertain hours.

Even so, as she heard his laughter and watched the small pink body wriggling delightedly in the water, she had a sudden fierce desire to snatch him up into her arms. So fierce, in fact, that it was almost as though she feared that in some way Rick was going to take Michael from her.

At that moment Rick looked up and saw her, and Kate flushed, wondering what it was he had seen in her eyes that made his own darken fractionally.

'You were late, so I thought I'd give Michael his bath.'

'Yes... Thank you.' She knew that her voice sounded strained, her thanks insincere. 'I'd better go and get ready. I take it Michael has had his supper?'

How shrewish and sharp she sounded, almost as though she wanted to find fault with him.

'At five o'clock,' Rick told her calmly. 'Shall I finish off here, or would you...'

Flushing angrily that he should so easily read the resentment in her eyes and know the cause of it, Kate shook her head and said tersely, 'Yes, if you would. I have to get changed. I'm being picked up at eight.'

'A dinner date?' Rick asked her.

Kate shook her head again.

'Not really. It's business.'

Michael, not happy with the fact that he had lost their attention, splashed noisily in his bath. Rick bent down to lift him out, wrapping him in a warm towel.

Feeling dismissed and shut out, Kate walked unsteadily into her own room. She had an absurd inclination to cry, something to do with the sight of Michael's chubby little arms wrapped so trustingly around the neck of the man holding him.

Once she must have been held like that by her father, but she could not remember it. What she could remember, though, was the pain that had come with knowing that her parents' love had been taken from her, and she had spent the rest of her life determined to make sure that she was never vulnerable to that kind of pain again, never allowing anyone close enough to her to cause her pain when they left her, never allowing herself the indulgence of physical contact with others. Until Michael came into her life. And the worst thing of all was that she didn't know whom she envied the most: Rick for the way Michael nestled so trustingly in his arms, or Michael because he had the sure strength of Rick's arms around him.

All the time she was getting ready, she could hear the soft sounds of Rick getting Michael ready for bed; intimate, tender little sounds that caught at her heart and made it ache dangerously.

She was just stepping into her dress when Rick knocked on her bedroom door.

'What is it?' she called out, realising her mistake the moment he opened the door and walked in.

She saw his eyebrows rise as she struggled frantically to tug her dress on, her face flushed and hot with embarrassment as the fabric stuck over her hips where she had accidentally bunched it, leaving the whole of her upper body bare apart from her lacy bra.

'I didn't mean you to come in,' she told him angrily. 'What is it you want, Rick?'

Fear of her own vulnerability made her voice sharp; she knew she was over-reacting, and she could see that Rick knew it too. He must be able to see how uncomfortable she felt, yet he made no move to leave, and Kate felt a slow burn of colour wash her skin as he quite deliberately looked at her.

Long ago, in her days in the home, when she had been forced to share a large bedroom with other girls, she had no doubt thought nothing of dressing and undressing in front of others. But those others had been members of her own sex and, besides, it had been a long time ago.

Her privacy was something that Kate had guarded very protectively in the years that had followed, and to have someone standing in her bedroom, watching her while she struggled to conceal herself from him, made her shake with a mixture of fear and anger that made it impossible for her to untangle the fabric of her dress.

Close to tears of rage and misery, she cried out sharply, 'Will you please get out of my room? I'm trying to get dressed.'

'And not succeeding very well,' Garrick told her drily, crossing the room. Before she could stop him, he was at her side, saying, 'Here, let me help you.'

Kate couldn't have moved if she'd tried. Her entire body tensed and then shook, as though she was in the grip of a fatal palsy. She felt Rick take hold of her dress and gently ease it up into the curve of her waist so that the bunched fabric could fall free. She felt the silk slither of its lining flow smoothly over her hips and thighs.

Like someone in a trance, she remained mute and obedient as Rick eased the top of her dress upwards and away from her body so that she could slide her arms into the sleeves.

He moved behind her. She felt the coldness of the metal zip and then the warmth of his hands through the fabric as he ran it upwards, closing it.

'A business dinner... Which restaurant is he taking you to?' he asked casually as he fastened the hook and eye at the top of her dress.

The question took several seconds to penetrate. Kate felt almost as though she were drugged and unable to respond to anything with her normal speed. Even though he was no longer touching her she could still feel the imprint of his fingers against her skin.

'We aren't going to a restaurant,' Kate told him huskily. It was oddly difficult to form the words, her throat felt tight and sore.

'He's taking you to his flat?' She saw the hard face tighten, a shrewd, mocking smile curling his mouth. 'I see. So that's how you do business is it, Kate— oiling the wheels of success with a little skilful seduction?'

Kate reacted without thinking, raising her hand and slapping his face hard at the same time as she burst out furiously, 'No, it is not! How dare you suggest such a thing? How...'

The protest died in her throat as he took hold of her, the grey eyes blazing with an anger that threatened to match her own and exceed it, but there was no anger in his voice, as the hard fingers dug into her arms, and his mouth curled in mocking amusement as he told her, 'You're very naïve for a successful business woman, Kate. Don't you know that there's only one effective punishment a man can inflict on a woman who slaps him, and that it's this?'

She cried out as his head blotted out the light, but the sound was smothered under the hard pressure of his mouth.

It was the first time she had been kissed by a man so obviously experienced in the art that, despite her rage and fear, she discovered that her own lips were softening treacherously beneath his skilled assault; and, as though the very fact of their tremulous softness pleased him, he didn't let her go, but used his tongue and his teeth to give her the most explicit and thorough lesson in the art of turning the angry pressure of mouth against mouth into the kind of sensual devastation that rocked her self-confidence on its foundations.

Quite when her eyes closed and she went limp in his arms, allowing him to draw her so close to his body that her breasts were flattened against his chest and she could feel the heavy thud of his heart as though it beat within her own body, she didn't know. It was only the awareness of his voice in her ear as he stopped kissing her that brought her back to reality, her eyes opening slowly, the pupils hugely dark with arousal and bemusement. At some point he had slid his fingers into her hair, and now they massaged the back of her scalp lazily as he looked down into her face.

'Perhaps I owe you an apology, after all,' he told her softly, watching every tiny betraying expression that crossed her face as she realised what had happened. 'But naïveté is no protection against a man like James Cameron, you know, Kate.'

The instant she was free of him, all Kate's mental functions sprang back into action.

'How would you know anything about him?' she demanded belligerently.

Instantly his face hardened as it had done before, and she could see that she had angered him.

'What are you trying to say? That as a humble nanny, I'm hardly likely to be qualified to hold an opinion on a successful businessman like Cameron? I read the papers. He doesn't have a very good reputation.'

His mouth twisted slightly, and Kate had to dismiss the accusation hovering on her lips that he was jealous of James's success.

This was a man who wasn't jealous of anyone, she acknowledged, a little shocked at having to accept that this was so; a humble nanny was how Rick had described himself in a voice dry with some kind of concealed amusement, but there was nothing humble about him at all.

'How did you know it was James Cameron I'm having dinner with?' Kate demanded.

'You told me.' He shrugged powerful shoulders. 'How else could I have known?'

Kate frowned. She was reasonably sure she had not told him, but he was quite right. How *could* he have known, otherwise?

She was only just beginning to recover from the shock of his kiss. She would have to say something to him about it . . . to make it clear to him that it was an incident that was never to be repeated . . . to even demand an explanation of why it had happened in the first place, only she suspected she knew. The male sex could never resist an opportunity of reinforcing their superior strength to the female. She had always known that, and Rick had just proved that she was right.

She was torn between an urgent need to tell him that she was going to dismiss him, and her recognition of the fact that she could not do so without first making sure she had someone to replace him.

And then there was Michael to think of, and there was no getting away from the fact that Michael responded far better to Rick than he had done to any of his other nannies. She couldn't dismiss him, she already knew that and so, she suspected, did he . . . Which left her with only one avenue of self-defence.

Drawing herself up to her full height, she said coldly, 'If this is the way you behaved with your previous employer, I'm not surprised she thought you were sexually available, but let me make one thing clear to you here and now. If I want a lover, I'm perfectly capable of finding myself one.'

'I don't doubt it,' he told her gravely, thoroughly disconcerting her both with his words and the look he gave her. It was almost approaching being tender, and she recoiled from it as though he had hit her.

An unexpected wail from Michael's room disturbed them both.

'I'll go,' Rick told her.

She heard him soothing the wakeful child, and then close the door as he went downstairs. It was half-past seven. If she didn't hurry, she was going to be late.

Her hands trembled as she brushed her hair and put on her make-up. Everything Rick had said and done had reinforced her doubts about going to James's flat, but she had no other option.

It was five to eight when she eventually felt calm enough to go downstairs. She had left her presentation in the sitting-room, and she was stunned to see Rick studying it for all the world as though he had every right to do so.

'Just what do you think you're doing?' she fumed as she swept into the room. 'That is private...'

'Sorry,' he apologised to her with a brief smile. 'I was just interested to see what you were planning.'

'And now that you *have* seen it, are you any the wiser?' she asked sarcastically.

She saw the brief flash of anger darken his eyes, but before he could say anything the doorbell rang.

'That will be James,' Kate told him hurriedly. 'I must go.'

For some reason she didn't want the two men to confront one another. Confront? It was only as she snatched up her papers and dashed to the front door that she wondered at her somewhat Freudian choice of verb.

James drove a silver-grey Porsche. He had parked it next to the Ferrari, and he frowned a little as he ushered her past it and opened the passenger door of his Porsche.

'Wealthy neighbours?' he questioned as Kate thanked him.

She responded with a vague smile, not wishing to tell him the truth and not wanting to fib either, but luckily he seemed to assume that his assumption was right and did not refer to the Ferrari again.

James very obviously enjoyed all the trappings of his success: the suit he was wearing had not come from one of his own chain store retailers, Kate acknowledged, and nor had the expensive cotton shirt. And yet, to the media, James proclaimed himself to be very much a man of the people. Not that there was anything wrong with a successful person enjoying that success, but Kate didn't like the way James sometimes mocked the very people who had been responsible for his success.

As they drove to his flat he name-dropped continuously, something else she detested, and she wondered whether he was actually trying to impress her, or if it had simply become a habit he was no longer aware he had.

His apartment was in an elegant Georgian terrace of houses of Eaton Square, with a complicated series of security checks to be gone through before they could walk into the main hallway that serviced all the apartments.

James's was on the second floor. A square hallway decorated in off-white and black, and to Kate's eyes too stark and modern for the elegance of the building, gave way to a drawing-room decorated in the same modernistic colours and furnished with a good deal of off-white leather and steel. While she could appreciate its design, she wondered a little at anyone choosing it for such an inappropriate setting.

'I've arranged for my staff to leave dinner ready for us. The bathrooms here are all en suite, I'm afraid. The apartment doesn't boast a separate cloakroom. If you'd . . .'

Kate shook her head quickly, her nerve-ends prickling, not so much at his comment but at the way he was looking at her.

A very prettily arranged cold meal had been left for them in the dining-room, but Kate was too nervous to eat. Refusing more than a single glass of wine, she fought down her butterflies of impatience while James refilled his several times. Then he insisted on having an after-dinner brandy, while Kate toyed with a second cup of coffee she didn't really want.

Over dinner, every time she had tried to discuss her presentation, James had steered the conversation into more personal channels. Kate wasn't sure she was too happy with the emphasis he seemed to place on his questions about her personal life, and she was thoroughly on edge by the time the meal was over and they were able to move into his study to discuss her presentation.

Whatever his reputation with her sex might be, he was a very able businessman, Kate reminded herself as she sat down opposite him across the expanse of the stained ash desk.

Like the other rooms she had seen, this one too was very modern in its decoration and furniture. It also struck her as rather cold and clinical, and certainly it was the direct opposite of the illusion she had decided to create for his new chain of supermarkets.

Neither of them spoke as he read through her presentation. Kate because she was too nervous, and James because he was studying the work she had done.

'I'm impressed,' he told her when he had finished. And Kate had the impression that he was not just impressed, but surprised as well; that he had not for some reason expected her to produce something of such a high standard. 'Your suggestions are good...if perhaps a little on the high side cost-wise.'

She opened her mouth to speak, but he forestalled her, saying silkily, 'Kate, you're the kind of woman I admire very much indeed...my kind of woman. Together we could form a very mutually advantageous partnership, don't you think? Whichever agency I eventually recommend to my main board will be getting a very valuable contract indeed...in terms of money and status.

'You remind me of myself twenty years ago. Young, ambitious, clever. Clever enough to know that sometimes in order to succeed we all need to give that little extra something.' He looked at her and smiled lazily, supremely confident that he would get what he wanted.

Kate's heart was bounding. She had no difficulty at all in interpreting his comments. He was telling her that if she wanted the contract she was going to have to sleep with him. This was something she had come up against on only a handful of occasions before, and she had made it plain then as she intended to do now that there was no way she was going to barter sexual favours in return for getting someone's business.

She took a deep, steadying breath and, maintaining eye contact with him, interrupted smoothly before he could go any further, 'I'm glad you like the presentation, and I'm flattered that you should compare my ambition with your own, but I'm afraid when it comes to that "little something extra"—well that's not the way I do business.'

She stood up as she spoke, firmly gathering up her papers, refusing to either hurry or appear to be frightened. It was rather like dealing with an aggressive dog, she told herself mentally; if she didn't betray her panic, everything would be all right.

But James obviously wasn't used to being refused. The lazy smile disappeared, and he looked at her in furious disbelief.

'If you think you can push the price up by doing this, forget it. Come on, Kate. I know how these things are done. You want the contract. I want you.'

'It's not the way I do business,' she told him curtly.

'No, so I've heard.'

And, as she looked at him, Kate wondered how much of his desire for her was fuelled by a need to be able to say to others that he had succeeded where they had failed.

It made her feel sick inside. She knew there were still businessmen like James, but they were getting fewer and fewer as more and more women became successful. She had been warned, though, both by Camilla and by Rick Evans.

She had all her papers together now. She looked across the desk and said quietly, 'I think it's best if I leave. If you should change your mind about the terms of the contract, you know where you can contact me.'

'Change my mind?' he laughed mockingly. 'You'll be the one who'll be doing that, my dear. Face it...you need the contract far more than I need your presentation.'

His arrogance made Kate lose her temper, and without even thinking of the consequences she said furiously, 'There's no contract on earth that's worth the price you're asking.' And too late she realised what she had done as she saw his face change, the gloating expression giving way to one of hot dislike.

'You little bitch,' she heard him saying thickly. 'You're all alike, you so-called businesswomen. Trying to turn men into eunuchs. It's time someone taught you a lesson.'

And as he lunged toward her, trying to grab hold of her, Kate realised her danger. It was not just her he disliked and resented, it was all women like her who dared to invade his male world, who made him feel insecure and threatened.

Just in time she managed to evade his grasp, grabbing her papers from the desk and almost running across the room to tug open the door. She heard him following her; the heavy sound of his breathing like something out of a childhood nightmare.

Luckily the door to the hallway was open and she darted through it, hearing James curse as he tried to cut off her exit and bumped into one of the heavy leather chairs.

Her hands trembled as she unlocked the front door to the apartment and then darted down the stairs rather than ring for the lift.

In her haste to escape she had forgotten the security locks on the massive front door into the street, but as she emerged into the hallway the door opened and, ignoring the startled expressions of the couple coming in, she dashed outside, pausing to catch her breath and steady her heartbeat.

It was only then that she realised she had left both her coat and evening bag in James's apartment.

It was a freezing cold night, something she hadn't realised when he'd driven her here, and her dress was very fine wool. The pavement was damp, and she only realised as she stepped out of the protection of the doorway that it had started to sleet, stinging pellets of icy rain that burned her skin and soaked through her dress.

A taxi sped down the street, sending up a spray of ice-cold water to drench her from the knees down as it pulled sharply into the kerb. She stepped toward it, but the driver flicked on his engaged light.

There was no guarantee that James wouldn't pursue her out into the street, although she thought it was extremely unlikely, but now that her initial panic had eased Kate realised that she had no way of getting home other than walking, since her money was in her evening purse in his flat.

If Camilla had been home she could have rung her and begged for help, but she wasn't. There was only one thing for it, she decided grimly, squaring her shoulders. She would have to walk. At least that way she might be able to keep warm. She didn't. Before she was more than half-way there she was soaked to the skin, or so it felt, the ever increasing sleet now like tiny daggers against her chilled skin.

She slipped once, her flimsy high-heeled shoes sliding on the icy pavement, and the shock of falling made her cry out sharply, but there was no one to hear her. By the time she was on her feet again she was shaking as well as shivering, and in the streetlight she saw the smear of blood on her knee, her flesh white against the ripped black tights she was wearing. She had also scraped her hands, and the palms stung painfully.

Blinking back tears of shock and pain, she tried to walk as quickly as she could. Her ankle ached painfully when she put her full weight on it, but at least it supported her.

She had never been more glad of anything in her life than to reach the familiar turning to her own street. She was limping badly now, and if she had had the energy she suspected she would probably have been crying with exhaustion.

As she reached her own front door, she leaned blissfully against it, automatically reaching out for her handbag and her key. But of course she didn't have either.

It was too much...much, much too much. She leaned her cheek against the door and let the tears flow, beating frustratedly on the smooth painted surface with hands too chilled to ball into fists.

CHAPTER SEVEN

When the solid wood gave way beneath her, Kate was too cold and shocked to realise why or to care, and not even Rick's incredulous, 'Kate! My God, what's happened to you?' really reached her.

She took a step forward and then another, shivering like a soaked cat, wanting only to crawl upstairs and go to bed, but Rick was standing in the way and another step forward brought her up against the solid warmth of his body and somehow or other into his arms.

She made a muffled protest and tried to step backwards, but it was too late. His arms had locked round her, and anyway he was so blissfully warm and comforting to lean on that she really didn't want to move at all. Having had her token protest rejected, she was quite content to let him hold her.

It would be bliss to close her eyes and go to sleep where she stood, supported and warmed by the bulk of that male body, but it seemed that Rick wasn't going to let her.

She gave a faint cry of protest when he moved her away from his warmth so that he could look down into her face.

'What the hell happened to you?' he demanded roughly. 'Is Cameron responsible for this?'

The hard anger in his voice penetrated through the shroud of icy cold numbing her. Kate opened her eyes and focused hazily on him. His mouth was a grim, hard line that indented in a severe and authoritative way she couldn't recognise. Her gaze shifted focus to his eyes. They, too, held an unfamiliar expression. Flat and cold and very, very masculine.

'*Is* he, Kate?' he reiterated curtly.

She shook her head and told him huskily, 'No. At least, not directly... He didn't attack me, if that's what you mean.'

Just those few words exhausted her, and she let her eyes close so that she could blank out the male anger in his face. For some reason that she couldn't find the energy to analyse right there and then, she found it almost comforting that Rick should be so concerned.

It struck her rather vaguely that this was hardly the reaction of the dedicated self-sufficient woman she considered herself to be, but she was too exhausted to dwell on the conundrum of her untypical behaviour too deeply.

'So who did?' Rick persisted, shaking her gently when she squeezed her eyes tightly closed.

'No one,' she told him crossly, when she realised he wasn't going to let her lie down and go to sleep as she so desperately wanted to do until he had got his answer.

'I fell in the street...' She shivered and said plaintively, 'Rick, I'm cold. I want to go to bed. I want to get warm.'

'You're soaked through,' he told her roughly. 'Where's your coat?'

'I left it in James's apartment,' she told him, too exhausted to prevaricate.

Even behind her closed eyelids she could feel the penetrating demand of his concentration. Reluctantly she opened her eyes, obeying his unspoken command.

'All right . . . we had an argument. He told me he'd give us the contract for his PR work if I went to bed with him.' She grimaced bitterly. 'I told him that isn't the way I do business, and left.'

'Without your coat?'

'*Yes!*' she admitted bitterly. 'He made a lunge for me and I panicked. I left my coat and my evening bag in his apartment, but at least I brought the presentation back with me.'

She heard Rick curse under his breath, and didn't know whether his savage denunciation was for her or for James.

'I warned you what he was like,' he told her, grim-faced. 'God almighty, call yourself a businesswoman, and yet you walked into his trap like a fly into honey.'

His scorn penetrated the icy miasma of exhaustion and misery surrounding her. Kate jerked back in his arms, her eyes glittering with the onset of fever and tears.

'If you're trying to suggest that I allowed greed to blind me to reality . . .'

'Not greed,' Rick countered swiftly, 'but if I were to substitute ambition for greed, could you be as quick to deny the charge?'

Kate felt a hot stain spread over her body. His words came too close to home for comfort. She had always had her doubts about the wisdom of dealing with James, about the sense of dining alone with him in his apartment, but her desperate need to secure the contract had forced her to put her doubts to one side.

And now to have Rick so accurately pinpoint that fact made her feel both resentful and fiercely defensive.

'Of course you would say that—just because I'm a woman. Ambition in a man is something to be praised and admired, but let a woman evidence the same drive and suddenly the whole world wants to criticise her.

'Is it really so very wrong of me to want to make a success of the agency? Not just for my own sake, either. I've got Michael to think of, the girls I employ—and even if I didn't, I'd still want to succeed,' she told him fiercely. 'And I don't see why I should be ashamed of admitting it ... A woman has just as much right to want to achieve as a man.'

'Yes, she has,' Rick agreed sombrely. 'It can also be a lot harder to succeed ... or a lot easier ... depending on what she's prepared to do, to achieve success.'

Kate ached in every bone in her body. The last thing she wanted was to have an in-depth discussion on moral values here in her hallway, when she was freezing cold and soaking wet. In fact all she wanted was for Rick to open his arms so that she could walk into them and forget everything bar the blissful warmth and protection of his body.

This knowledge of her own weakness shocked her. For the first time in her adult life she wanted something from another human being.

It was Michael who had caused her to develop this weakness. Michael, whose dependence and love had pierced the invulnerable wall she had built around herself, Michael who had destroyed that barrier with his dependence and need and left her vulnerable to emotions she had promised herself she would never feel.

She knew all about the dangers of loving others...the pain of the loss...the loneliness of being part of a close knit unit that had disintegrated. She had experienced it all when she lost her parents and she told herself all through her growing up years that she was never going to experience it again. And the best way to do that was not to allow anyone close to her; not to allow herself to want anyone to be close to her. So why was she now aching for Rick to stop lecturing her and instead to enfold her in his arms and comfort her with tenderness and care?

She couldn't ignore his statement though, nor the challenge it contained. It had to be answered.

She lifted too heavy eyelids and focused on him with difficulty:

'If you're saying that life will always be easier for those women who are prepared to barter sex for favours, then yes, I agree with you that in the past that was the case, but that's changing. Women are no longer prepared to sell themselves short. They no longer need to.' Her head lifted proudly, her eyes glittering with more than the fire of the fever she was holding at bay. 'If you're trying to suggest that I might have at any time considered sleeping with James in order to secure the contract, then you're quite wrong. That isn't the way I do business, and it never will be.'

'No,' Garrick agreed quietly. 'I can see that.'

He ought to be feeling angry; if he could prove that she was the type of woman who slept around, who sold herself to gain business advantages, it would be easier for him to prove her an unfit guardian for

Michael, but instead, what he did feel was a rush of satisfaction and relief that his judgement had not been at fault, coupled with an urgent and very masculine desire to seek out James Cameron and make him pay for every second of discomfort and fear Kate had experienced. And there had been fear. He had seen it flash briefly through her eyes, even though she had tried to deny it.

As she closed her eyes again and swayed where she stood, he suddenly became aware of everything that his furious anxiety had made him ignore. She was freezing, her teeth chattering, her wet clothes clinging to her like a second skin, while a thin blue line of extreme cold whitened the flesh round her mouth. He cursed himself for keeping her standing in the small, cold hall when she so desperately needed to get warm and dry.

Her eyes closed, unable to read the contrition and guilt in his eyes, Kate shivered and protested huskily, 'I don't want to talk any more. I'm cold.' She tried to walk past him and head for the stairs, but her fall had damaged her ankle more than she realised, and having stood still for so long the torn muscles had stiffened up and refused to support her, so that the moment she tried to move she fell forward with a sharp cry of panic, remembering how it had felt to land on the hard pavement.

But, blissfully, this time she didn't fall; she was instead scooped up into strong arms. The realisation that she was back in Rick's arms made her give a small betraying murmur of contentment that drew his gaze to her white face and closed eyes. A faint frown touched his forehead. The situation was already difficult enough, without any further complications. It struck him as grimly amusing that he should be able to remain immune to the experienced advances of any amount of worldly and beautiful women, and yet the moment he had Kate in his arms his body refused to respond to a single one of his commands to ignore its sexual response to her. Not even as a teenager had he reacted like this. Sex was an enjoyable experience, but desire had never touched him with such sharp necessity that he could scarcely think beyond making love to the woman in his arms.

As he supported her weight, he fought to inject the right note of calm distance into his voice as he told her, 'Kate, you're soaking. You need to get undressed and have a hot bath. Can you manage to do that?'

With her eyes closed, Kate felt the full force of the message of her other senses; all of them registered Rick's tension, told her of his grim dislike of holding her, and she remembered that he had left his previous employment due to the unwanted sexual advances of the woman whom he worked for.

Was that what he feared now? That she was going to make advances to him, that her exhaustion was simply a ploy to lure him into bed with her? She shivered with distaste at the thought of humiliating herself in such a way.

'Of course I can manage,' she lied. 'Perhaps if you'd put me down, I could prove it to you.'

Something dark and intimidating flashed in his eyes, and he set her down so quickly that her whole body jarred with pain.

'You're always so eager to maintain that distance you keep between yourself and the rest of the world, aren't you, Kate? That fierce independence of yours, that refusal to allow yourself to admit that you are human . . . that there are occasions when you can't be wholly self-sufficient. Why?' he demanded with un-expected harshness. 'What's happened in your life to make you refuse to admit that you can be vulnerable just like the rest of us . . . Was it a man?' he hazarded.

His questions, so shockingly intimate and direct, coming on top of her fear and physical exhaustion, somehow or other got through the defences she nor-mally erected against such enquiries. She stared at him blindly, trying to breathe evenly and failing as her body betrayed her.

'No. It wasn't a man,' she told him slowly, and with the words came another kind of pain: the bitter sweetness of memories she had tried to forget for too long. Memories of her early childhood, when she had been happy . . . loved . . . when she had never known the harsh reality that life could be.

Rick saw the pain come into her eyes and found he was holding his own breath, willing her to confide in him, to share with him whatever it was that had made her close herself up in defences so tightly cast that in normal circumstances she would allow nothing to breach them.

Tonight he had caught her off guard, had almost trapped her into self-revelation, and as he watched her he fought down the compunction and guilt that threatened to make him back off with his questions unanswered.

'No, it wasn't a man,' she repeated slowly, looking not at him but past him, her eyes huge and shadowed, as though she were focusing something beyond his sight . . . something only she could see . . . 'It was my parents.'

He felt the shock bolt through him. Her parents! He didn't understand. According to his reports, they had died when she was a child . . . and then suddenly he knew. Compassion filled him. He touched her arm, and as though in some way his touch communicated to her his feelings, she turned and looked at him and said gravely, in a childlike way, 'They left me, you see... And I...' Tears flooded her eyes and she pushed half-heartedly at their overflow, much in the way a child might. 'I had to go and live in a children's home. I couldn't understand what had happened at first. I kept on thinking that it was all a mistake. That they weren't dead really, and that they would come for me.' She gave a tense shudder. 'Some days I felt I hated them because they'd left me.'

'They couldn't help it, Kate,' Rick told her gently.

'I know that,' she told him with a trace of impatience. 'I knew it then, but can't you see . . . even though I knew it wasn't their fault, some part of me couldn't help blaming them for leaving me behind . . . They should have taken me with them, and then we'd . . .'

'Kate, no!' Rick interrupted her harshly . . . so harshly that she focused properly on him, and suddenly realised what she was doing, what she was saying . . .

'Of course, I didn't really want to die . . . Not after the first few months, but if it hadn't been for Jen . . .'

'Michael's mother?' Rick interrupted gently. Her eyes had become soft and unfocused again, as though she was physically looking back into the past and witnessing again its pains.

'Yes. She sort of adopted me at the children's home ... mothered me in a way. Without her....' She broke off and looked at him. 'That's why I cherish my independence, Rick ... that's why it's so important to me. Because I learned young how vulnerable needing other human beings makes you ... They go away and leave you alone ... in pain ... Loving causes pain.'

'Therefore it's better not to love at all,' Rick supplemented softly for her. 'Better not to care, or to become involved ... better not to allow anyone inside that fortress you've built around your heart. There's only one flaw in that argument,' he added softly, and when she looked at him in tense watchfulness he asked, 'What about Michael? And don't tell me you don't love him, Kate.'

'Michael's different,' she told him wildly. 'I owed it to Jen to ...'

'Love her son? Ah, I see ... so it's all right for you to love where that love is a duty ... is that what you're saying?'

Suddenly Kate didn't know what she was saying any more. Or what she was feeling, other than an odd feeling of suddenly having put down an enormous burden.

Her independence, a burden? Her almost ceaseless striving to make her life free of any kind of emotional ties, a burden? It wasn't possible ... was it?

'Man does not live by independence alone,' Rick told her drily, deliberately misquoting. 'And neither does woman, or should I say, most especially woman does not.'

'That is one of the most sexist remarks I've ever heard,' Kate snapped at him, glad of something to focus her feelings on, glad to have some excuse to recover from the shock of having confided in him so readily...so almost wantonly gladly, she acknowledged bitterly.

'You misunderstood me,' Rick told her calmly. 'Men and women both have their separate strengths and weaknesses. The male sex has a long way to go before its emotions are as well tuned as the female. Don't deny yourself those emotions, Kate. They're what make...'

'Women so vulnerable!' she snapped at him.

'Men are vulnerable, too,' he told her. 'Not all women are as honest as you, as I discovered the hard way as a young and very naïve man.'

Now it was his turn to look confused and frown, as though bewildered by the way he had confided in her and admitted his vulnerability.

Kate was surprised as well, and—yes, flattered, she acknowledged, while mentally berating herself for being so predictably female.

And yet his confidence had been no male ploy. It had been spontaneous and honest. She had an insane desire to reach out and touch him, and both it and the fear it brought showed briefly on her face. She withdrew from him, half stumbling as she started to move away.

She heard Rick curse, but he made no move to touch her, and that sensitivity to her feelings made her whole body prickle warningly. This man was dangerous to her, dangerous in ways that she was only just beginning to be able to calculate. He drew responses from her, both verbal and physical, she would never normally have dreamed of giving... made her feel things she had no desire to feel... made her see things both about herself and him she had no wish to see...

'I'll go and make you a hot drink,' she heard him saying curtly, and Kate tried to convince herself that she wasn't experiencing a sharp sense of loss as he turned his back on her and walked into the kitchen.

She winced as she limped painfully across the hall, and by the time she had reached the top of the stairs, despite the icy chill in the rest of her body, her ankle felt as though it were on fire, throbbing agonisingly with every step she took.

Once inside her bedroom, she didn't even bother to turn on the light, dragging herself over to the bed and almost falling on to it. She lay there, alternately shivering and sweating, drifting in and out of an awareness that kept urging her to do something important, but she couldn't quite reach out and grasp what it was. Her ankle and calf hurt... She reached down to ease off her shoe to soothe the pain, her mind clouded by the trauma of the evening and the onset of exhaustion, so that she was only half aware of the swelling round the ankle and the hot fire of her skin.

She wanted to get undressed and have a shower, but it was too much of an effort. She was cold and she knew that she ought to remove her wet clothes and get beneath the bedclothes, but she simply couldn't find the strength, so instead she gave in to the exhaustion numbing her and closed her eyes.

At first when Rick walked into the bedroom he thought she was still in her bathroom, and then in the streetlight that illuminated the room he saw her lying on the bed, the light streaming in, highlighting her swollen ankle.

He put down the drink he had made and went over to the bed, quickly examining the swollen flesh. Despite his care, Kate muttered and winced, opening pain-hazed eyes.

Rick was looking at her with a mixture of ire and consternation. She tried to sit up, instinctively seeking to defend herself against a pity she didn't want by pretending that she was all right, but the movement jarred her ankle and made her cry out.

I'm going to call your doctor,' Rick announced curtly, stepping back from the bed.

A doctor was the last thing Kate wanted. All she needed was to be allowed to go to sleep so that she could get warm and forget the traumas of the evening.

'No,' she argued. 'It isn't necessary.'

A violent shivering fit accompanied her denial, her teeth starting to chatter. 'I just want to go to sleep and get warm,' she added under her breath, whimpering slightly as she tried to move and jarred her foot.

Her ankle was sprained and not broken, Rick acknowledged, and she was probably right, warmth and sleep were probably more important to her right now than a doctor.

'All right,' he agreed, giving in. 'Don't try to move. I'll run a bath for you and then come back for you.'

'No!' Kate protested sharply, halting him with the vehemence of her rejection. 'I can manage.'

Garrick looked into her white face and saw the stubborn firming of her chin. She was different from any other woman he had known, her stubborn independence both irritating and unnecessary.

Walking back over to the bed, he leaned over her and said levelly, 'I'm almost tempted to let you try, but we both know you couldn't even get as far as the door on that ankle.'

'If you'd let me come upstairs the moment I got in instead of cross-questioning me, I'd have been perfectly all right,' she fibbed, glaring at him, her defiant stance spoiled by the sudden fit of shivering that convulsed her.

Grim-mouthed, Rick headed for the bathroom door, and she could hear him running water into the bath.

She felt as weak as a kitten, boneless and completely unable to move. She knew she ought to be doing something, taking off her wet clothes perhaps and putting on her robe, but it made her head ache just to think of so much painful activity. It was much, much easier to simply close her eyes and let the sound of the running water soothe her. She imagined herself lying in it, lapped in luxury and warmth, and she gave another shiver, unpleasantly conscious of her damp clothes and cold skin.

'Kate.'

The curt voice so close to her ear made her flinch. Rick had moved so quietly, she hadn't heard him come back in. She opened her eyes and stared at him with confused uncertainty.

'Bath's ready,' he told her in a clipped voice.

She started to sit up and found that her muscles were simply too weak to respond, leaving her to flop inelegantly back on to the mattress.

'Here, drink this,' Rick ordered, lifting a mug to her lips.

A strong smell of brandy assailed her, making her gasp and push the mug away.

'I'm not drinking that.'

'Oh, yes, you are,' Rick retorted grimly. 'It probably smells worse than it tastes; hot milk laced with brandy, that's all it is. It will warm you up and help you sleep.'

'I don't want it,' Kate told him petulantly, gasping with shock when Rick suddenly put the mug down on the table beside her bed, and then hauled her into a sitting position, ignoring her angry protests and then firmly imprisoning both her hands at her sides simply by circling one arm around her, leaving him free to use the other to lift the mug to her lips and say savagely, 'Drink it!'

Sensing that to refuse would only prolong her humiliation, Kate opened her mouth and obediently took a swallow. She gasped as the spirit burned her throat, making her choke and splutter, but Rick ignored her protests and refused to give up until she had almost drained the mug.

She had no idea how much brandy had been in the milk, but already she felt dizzy and light-headed. So much so that she was barely aware of the fact that her arms were free and that Rick was briskly unzipping her dress, until she felt the warmth of the centrally heated air against her cold, damp skin.

As she tensed, as though sensing what she was going to say, Rick told her harshly, 'Both of us know you're in no fit state to do this yourself, Kate, and I hope both of us know that I'm not about to take advantage of the situation.'

He had difficulty steadying his hands as he made that second statement. The truth was that he was already affected far more than was safe, and it didn't matter how much he told himself to be clinical and detached, his body flagrantly ignored his commands to deny its awareness of her.

'No, and *I'm* not your last employer,' Kate muttered breathlessly as he moved her gently so that he could slide the damp dress down over her hips.

'Right,' Rick agreed tonelessly. 'Now that we've both agreed that neither of us is in the least danger of being seduced, perhaps we can get on with the task of getting you bathed and into bed.'

Busy trying to analyse just why the odd roughness that had entered his voice should send such a frisson of sensation spiralling down her spine, Kate didn't realise quite how literally he meant his comment, until she discovered that he was unfastening her bra and peeling the damp silk away from her skin.

She was lying on her front, but even so a hot, fierce surge of heat turned her pale skin scarlet, her head lifting so that she could look over her shoulder at him and hiss frantically, 'That's enough! I can do the rest myself.'

'Is that right? Then how come I found you flat out here still in your wet clothes? I admire your modesty, Kate, but there's a time and place for everything, and this isn't it.' His hands rested loosely on her hips. She could feel their warmth through the thin silk of her panties.

'You don't have anything I haven't seen before, you know,' he told her half mockingly, and as she jerked round to glare furiously at him he took advantage of the movement to grip hold of both her briefs and tights, easing them past the feminine curve of her hips before she realised what was happening.

He had never been an indiscriminate lover, and was accredited with far more partners than there had actually been, but there had certainly been enough for the female body not to be a mystery to him any longer, and yet there was something about Kate's...something about the shadowed mystery of the narrow curve of her waist; the soft swell of her stomach, held taut in nervous dread and quivering just slightly; the gentle mound between her thighs that was clothed in soft shadow; the defensive angling of her body, that moved him almost unbearably.

Tense and watchful, Kate could feel the embarrassed heat spreading through her. She had never paid much attention to her own body, never compared it with those of other women, because there had never been any need. Since she had no intention of loving anyone or sharing her life with them, she had had no need to look at her body in the light of its appeal to a man. Now she wondered whether Rick's stillness was caused by revulsion or amusement.

She started to shake violently and not because she was cold.

'What's wrong?' Rick demanded softly.

'Stop looking at me like that.'

'Like what?' he queried, tensing.

'Like I'm some kind of...of inferior specimen of my species,' Kate said wildly.

His head turned slightly and his glance locked with hers; alert and dangerous. 'Is that what you thought? You couldn't be more wrong. I've never seen anything more perfect in my life.'

And as she started to protest that he was lying, his hands cradled her hips and he bent his head and gently kissed her quivering stomach not just once but several times, until his lips came to rest for the briefest fraction of time just above the soft rise of flesh that protected her womanhood.

'Perfect,' he repeated in a hoarse, unsteady voice, and then he released her and stood up abruptly, picking her up in his arms before she could formulate a single word of protest, saying flatly, 'That bath water's going to be cold.'

It wasn't, but Kate was quite certain that nothing could feel as hot as her skin where his lips had caressed it. What on earth had made him do it? Had he felt sorry for her? Was that it? It must have been, because he certainly didn't desire her.

He refused to leave the bathroom, but at least allowed her to wash herself, and she sank beneath the water in a belated attempt to hide her nudity from him. Unaware that her thoughts were quite clearly visible on her face, she froze as she heard him say, 'You're wrong, you know. I do desire you, and don't even think about looking for proof. The way I feel right now, there's nothing I want more than to take you to bed and make love to you all night and to hell with the consequences.'

Too stupefied to say a word, Kate could only give him the odd covert glance as she struggled to finish her ablutions. Was she dreaming or had Rick just said that he desired her?

She gave him a brief glance from beneath lowered lashes and heard him swear softly. 'Don't push me, Kate,' he warned her harshly. 'The last thing you need right now is me in your bed, but that's exactly what you're going to get if you keep on giving me those curious little looks.'

She glared at him, and he laughed grimly,

'OK, go ahead and glare at me if you wish, but you're looking at me as though you'd love to know what my body would feel like over yours, and if you don't stop it, I promise you you're all too likely to find out.'

Quite how she would have responded, Kate didn't know, but a violent fit of sneezing saved her the trouble, and before she could protest Rick had lifted her out of the water and wrapped her in a huge warm bath towel.

'I think for the sake of my health as well as your own, the sooner you're tucked up in bed, the better,' he told her huskily. 'Can you manage to dry yourself while I go downstairs and fill a hot-water bottle for you?'

Kate nodded. In fact, she felt weaker than ever, but she dared not tell him so in case he thought she was inviting him to make love to her.

But what if she did? Would it really be the end of the world—the end of her self-respect? Wasn't she entitled to relax the tight control she had kept over herself for once in her life? After all, they would not be hurting or harming anyone...neither of them owed any commitment to anyone else, and if she knew that

Rick could only be a brief interlude in her life, that didn't stop the fierce ache inside her that his soft warmings had aroused.

She wanted him to make love to her, she recognised on a thrill of shock. For the first time in her life she was experiencing the reckless, heady drive of desire...the need to fulfil her female destiny, the urge to surrender her independence and know the dangerous thrill of loving another human being.

Loving. She tensed, her muscles locking. Rick had been talking about sex, not love. *Love* was what she felt for Michael, and had nothing to do with the fierce clamour in her senses that Rick aroused.

Physical desire could play dangerous tricks on the unwary; and that was all she felt for Rick—physical desire. There was nothing else. There could not be anything else.

By the time he returned with her hot-water bottle, she had managed to stagger painfully back to bed. She took the hot-water bottle from him with a cool thank you. It was better this way, she assured herself as he left the room. Better, wiser, safer. So why did she wish she had been born a different person? The kind of person who could have subtly and freely indicated that there was no need for them to sleep alone. She would feel better in the morning, she promised herself. She would be glad then that she had acted the way she had.

CHAPTER EIGHT

BUT she wasn't, not really. When she woke up in the morning still drowsy from sleep, Kate wasn't sure what had caused the small ache low down in the pit of her stomach. She rolled instinctively on to her stomach, trying to banish it, and then abruptly turned over and shot upright, a wave of heat crawling over her skin as she realised just exactly what the ache was.

Furious with herself for what she saw as a weakness in her defences, she got out of bed, refusing to wince as her still swollen ankle twinged painfully.

She could walk on it—just about, she told herself grimly as she half hobbled, and half dragged herself to her bathroom.

She dressed in a full, soft wool skirt with which she could wear boots which would both disguise the swelling and give her ankle some much needed support. It was a struggle getting them on, and at the back of her mind lay the knowledge that she was behaving both foolishly and irresponsibly. She would be much wiser simply acknowledging the fact that she had hurt herself and working at home for a couple of days.

But she couldn't do that. Now that they had lost any chance of getting James's contract, she was going to have to work doubly hard just to bring in enough money to cover her commitments. As she checked her make-up, she berated herself mentally for her folly in not handling James better. If she hadn't panicked, if she had used a bit of tact...a bit of flattery...

A brisk rap on her bedroom door stemmed the flood of guilt. She called out coolly, 'Come in,' not wanting to admit even to herself how hard she was having to struggle to suppress the faint fluttering of tension in her stomach.

Rick came in, carrying Michael, and a mug of coffee.

He frowned when he saw that she was dressed and out of bed. He himself was wearing jeans and a soft woollen checked shirt with the sleeves rolled back, revealing the muscled hardness of his forearm.

Michael nestled sleepily in the crook of his arm, obviously more than content to be with him, and she had a sharp pang of dark resentment. She should be the one holding Michael.

She was jealous, she recognised miserably. Jealous of the fact that Michael had settled down so well with his new nanny. Was this how other working mothers felt when the time came to return to their work and leave their child in the care of someone else? The violence of her feelings confused her. She loved Michael, but he was surely incidental to her life? A responsibility she had taken on and would do her best for, yes—but it was her career that was the focal point of her life, surely?

Was it? If it had been, wouldn't she have tried harder last night to placate James? Wouldn't she surely have refused to flinch at his proposition and dealt with it in a far more professional and judicious way?

'I don't believe I'm seeing this,' Rick commented brusquely, interrupting her thoughts. 'Don't tell me you actually mean to go into your office? For God's sake, woman, have you no sense? You're in no fit state.'

How long had it been since anyone had expressed this kind of tough male concern for her? How long had it been since she had experienced a very feminine responsiveness to it? Not since her parents had died, surely? That knowledge frightened her; she felt as though she had suddenly stepped on to very treacherous ground and was quickly being sucked down into the trap of its dangers. Emotionalism was the weakness that always trapped her sex, that deflected it from its course; and it was a weakness which men had exploited callously for their own benefit for hundreds of generations. Well, no one was going to exploit her.

'I think that's for me to decide, don't you?' she told him crisply.

She dared not look at him, no matter how in control she sounded. She was all too conscious of the held-in irritation emanating from him, the very male impatience with what he no doubt considered to be her very feminine stupidity.

'Take Michael downstairs and give him his breakfast, will you, please, Rick?' she requested with crisp efficiency, still refusing to look at him. 'I want to get an early start today. I've rather a lot to do.'

With unerring and very unnerving accuracy, he seemed to read her thoughts, because he didn't move but instead said derisively, 'Like getting in touch with

Cameron to apologise for running out on him last night?'

Kate couldn't help it, her skin burned dark red. How had he known that had been in her mind?

The look of contempt in his eyes quite clearly betrayed what he thought of her. She wanted to cry out to him that he didn't understand, that he had no idea of the financial pressure she was under...that he didn't realise how important this contract was to her, and to Michael.

'Is that what you're going to do?' he demanded softly.

She was too taken aback to chastise him for the question. The very intensity of the biting sneer in his voice made her face him, her own head lifting, her eyes bright with challenge.

'I don't think that's any concern of yours, do you?'

'Having second thoughts about those ethics of yours, Kate?'

She flinched beneath the quiet words, hardly noticing the familiar way in which he used her Christian name. Suddenly it had become very important to make him see the justification for what she must do.

'Last night I panicked,' she told him huskily. 'I behaved foolishly, unprofessionally.'

'I see. So this time you're going to handle it differently, is that it? This time you're going to let him blackmail you into going to bed with him, is that it?'

'No!'

His grim mouth relaxed a little as she made the instinctive denial.

'You're deluding yourself if you think he's going to accept anything else,' he told her, and in an illuminating moment of self-awareness Kate realised that he was right. Last night she had dealt a blow to James's pride that only her complete capitulation and humiliation would salve.

Wearily her shoulders sagged, her despair shadowing her eyes as she stared out of the window. Last night she had lost her golden chance. She had panicked and thrown it away as carelessly as an unknowing child, and all because she couldn't bear the thought of James touching her.

'I could have handled it differently.'

She said the words more to herself than to Rick Evans, but he caught them and scoffed. 'How? By letting him think you were going to bed with him and then pulling out at the last minute? Is that how you want to do business, Kate?'

It wasn't and she shivered, not liking the image he was drawing for her.

'I've got to get into the office,' she told him tonelessly, and she knew from the flatness of her voice that he had guessed that what he had said had forced her to abandon her plans for making contact with James. He had made her see all too clearly that there was no way back. She had had her chance and she had blown it. Fate might not be inclined to favour her again. And if it wasn't... If it wasn't, she could lose everything she had worked for, she acknowledged painfully.

She moved abruptly, wincing as her ankle twinged. Now that she was up and dressed she felt oddly weak, and not just because of her ankle, either. There was an ominous tickly sensation at the back of her throat, and she kept on having to suppress the urge to shiver.

'I must go,' she announced, and was appalled to discover how hoarse her voice sounded.

A cold was the last thing she needed right now. She saw Rick frown, and for one vulnerable moment she almost wished that he would announce that he wasn't going to let her. She must be hallucinating if she was having thoughts like that, she told herself furiously.

'Has Michael got something that can go in the car?'

The abrupt question startled her, and for a moment she wasn't quite sure what Rick meant.

'A carry cot or something, that will keep him safe while I run you to the office. I'd let you take the Ferrari, but with that foot, I'm damn sure you'd never get it out of first gear.'

Take the Ferrari? Her eyes widened slightly, and then hard on the heels of the realisation of how blissful it would be to simply sit back and let Rick take charge, came the panicky knowledge of how dangerous such a weakness would be. She had not fought for all her adult years to preserve her independence and invulnerability simply to throw it all away now just because her head ached and her ankle throbbed.

'I can get a cab.'

'There's no need. Can you make it downstairs, by the way, or . . .'

'Of course I can.'

But she wasn't as confident as she sounded, and so to distract him she told him where he could find the carry cot that fastened into the back seat of a car.

A merely adequate driver herself, she was impressed by the sure way Rick handled the powerful Ferrari. He had just that powerful blending of control and flair that could perhaps be described as macho, although Kate hesitated to choose such an over-used description.

She was surprised that Rick seemed to know exactly how to find her office without her having to give him any directions. He stopped the car and then courteously helped her out, and she needed the firm support of his hand beneath her arm, she recognised, as she tried not to shiver when the cold morning air touched her heated skin.

It occurred to her that she might possibly have the beginnings of a slight fever, but she pushed the thought away, not wanting to have to handle yet another burden. She had enough problems as it was, and as though he knew what was in her mind, Rick said firmly, 'When you came home last night, I admired you for the stand you had taken, Kate. Not many people nowadays have such a strong set of values. Don't be deceived into thinking that they don't matter, because they do. You'll be the person who'll suffer the most if you abandon them, because you're one of those rare people whose own good opinion of themselves matters more than any fawning flattery from others.'

What he was saying was quite true, but she was amazed that he had recognised that stubborn pride within her, which she privately resented, and which had kept her aloof and immovable from the code of ethics she had chosen for herself. Ethics which she was slowly beginning to realise it was going to be costly to hold on to.

'The world isn't made up of men like Cameron,' Rick added quietly, almost reassuringly, she recognised, as he continued to hold her arm, firmly supporting her.

'It isn't full of good contracts, either,' she told him crisply, not wanting to give in to the pleasure of letting his concern for her wrap round her like a warm comforter. It was weak to want to cling to his reassurance, to want to cling to him. It was because she wasn't feeling well, because last night had re-opened some of the wounds of the past, because James's touch had made her remember the horror and disgust she had felt as a teenager when one of the boys at the home had tried to molest her. Rick's touch, on the other hand, aroused none of those feelings of disgust and dislike. When Rick touched her...

'There'll be other contracts,' he assured her, holding her gaze with his, as though he was willing her to take courage and believe what he was telling her. 'And they'll be all the better for coming after what you experienced last night, because they'll be contracts from people who respect you for the kind of woman you are.'

'For the kind of *person* I am, don't you mean?' Kate corrected bitterly, not wanting him to know how affected she was by his quiet assurances. 'I don't want any of my business contacts to see me as a woman. I want to be judged on equal terms with them. And as for the other contracts—well, I hope you're right, Rick, otherwise you could well find yourself without a job in a very short space of time indeed.''

It was the first time she had ever allowed anyone bar Camilla to see how much her financial insecurity worried her. She had often heard successful people claiming that the days when they had struggled for success had been among the most pleasurable and challenging of their lives, but that was in retrospect, and often said when they had had a partner, a lover, someone to share the hard times with.

She had no one, and she also had the responsibility of Michael. She had initially enjoyed the challenge of setting up on her own, but now, with the knowledge that she had lost James's contract, she felt sick at heart, chilled to the bones and infinitely weary. So weary that she would have given anything to simply lie down, close her eyes and go to sleep... to forget her cares, and escape from them.

But she couldn't do that, and so, giving Rick a tight little smile, she stepped away from him and toward the building that housed her office.

As he got back in the Ferrari, Garrick checked on Michael, who was staring interestedly around him.

'Well, now,' he told the serious-eyed little boy. 'You and I have work to do.' And, instead of turning the car in the direction of Kate's home, he drove to the prestigious block that housed the headquarters of the Evans Gould Corporation.

John Gould, who had been his partner when he originally bought his first company, had now retired, having sold out his share of the business to Garrick, but Garrick had retained the original title, thinking it less confusing than making a change.

He drove the Ferrari into his personal car parking space, and then lifted Michael out of the back. If the staff thought it odd to see their chairman striding through the building dressed in worn jeans and a shirt instead of his normal Savile Row suits, carrying instead of his briefcase a small brown-haired child, they were far too well trained to betray it.

Only the receptionist on the floor that contained the directors' boardroom and Garrick's personal office widened her eyes in amazement and stared at her august boss in obvious confusion.

'Mr Evans,' she stammered hesitantly, 'Mr Oswald told us that you wouldn't be coming in. Er...shall I get you some coffee?'

'Yes, please, Amanda, and—er...some milk, please, as well. But first I want you to ring through to Gerald and tell him to come up and see me.'

His assistant arrived within five minutes, plainly as surprised as the receptionist to see Garrick, but rather better at concealing it.

Garrick had put Michael down on the floor, and he was enjoying himself crawling about and trying to eat the legs of the very expensive rosewood desk.

'I know we've got a lot on, Gerald,' Garrick told him. 'But I've got an urgent job for you. Something that must be kept completely confidential. I don't want anyone here at Evans Gould to know anything about this. Is that clear?'

When Gerald had nodded in affirmation, he said crisply, 'I want a comprehensive list of all the companies in the group who use or need to use a PR agency. I want details of the agencies used, the performance results and how long the contracts already in existence are due to run.'

He saw that Gerald was looking at him rather curiously. 'I'm thinking of trying a new agency.'

He saw the brief flash of comprehension darken his assistant's eyes, and wondered rather drily if Gerald had the slightest idea what was really in his mind. Probably not . . . which was just as well.

Michael, bored with the lack of interesting things to play with, turned to look at the two men and started to cry, holding out his arms to Garrick once he had caught his attention.

'Had enough, have you? All right.' And picking up the little boy with easy confidence he apologised to the receptionist as she walked in with a tray of coffee and milk.

'Sorry, Amanda, I haven't time to drink it, after all. Oh, and I want that information just as soon as you can organise it, Gerald. OK?'

It said a great deal for the respect with which his staff viewed their chairman that, after he had gone, not one of them who had seen him saw any necessity to speculate openly on exactly what was going on.

By lunch time, Kate's head was aching so much she could barely see, never mind think. She was suffering from alternate bouts of shivering fits and hot sweats.

A messenger had arrived half-way through the morning from James, returning her coat and evening bag, and, seeing the speculation in Sara's eyes as she brought the things in to her office, she had felt obliged to let the other girl know that they would not be getting the contract.

Dispirited and exhausted, she was in no condition to fight off what threatened to be an ill-timed bout of 'flu, she recognised as the faint discomfort at the back of her throat gave way to a full-blown jagged mountain past which it felt impossible to swallow.

Almost light-headed with fever, she struggled over the columns of figures she was desperately trying to add up. Her emergency reserves were so pitifully small, scarcely more than a month, two months' outgoings at the most. If she didn't get some new clients very quickly...

She closed her eyes, not wanting to even think the words.

At half-past one her telephone rang. She picked up the receiver shakily and croaked her name into it. There was a brief silence, and then Rick's voice saying drily, 'Obviously I don't need to ask how you're feeling. Why don't you call it a day and come home?'

Beyond her shock that as her employee he should speak to her so arrogantly was a weak longing to either burst into tears or beg him to come and fetch her.

Her eyes felt scratchy and dry; her throat was a fiery torment; her body was weak from the spasmodic bursts of shivers that racked it. She ached from her head to her foot, and her ankle was barely carrying her weight. Add to that the pounding headache that was not just a result of her tussle with her accounts, and she had every reason to feel weak and tearful, logic told her, but she couldn't accept that logic. That need she had just experienced to rely on someone else was like a terrifying pit opening up at her feet, a much feared nightmare suddenly come to life. She must not allow herself to be weak, to be anything other than self-sufficient. She dared not. She had suffered once in her life through losing those she had loved; she couldn't endure that kind of pain again. Some children in the same situation became desperately anxious to replace their lost parents and clung fearfully to any adult they could; she had been the opposite, standing proud and alone, and that was how she intended to live her whole life.

'Kate,' Rick urged her, and she gripped the receiver hard, refusing to give in to what she knew to be the most sensible course of action.

'What was it you wanted?' she asked him hoarsely. 'Is there something wrong with Michael?'

She heard his brief indrawn breath of irritation. 'No,' he told her drily. 'Unlike you, Michael is in perfect health.'

'Then I'm afraid I must go. I'm rather busy.'

She replaced the receiver, dismayed to discover how much she was shaking. So much so, in fact, that she hardly dared let go of the instrument.

She got up and walked blindly toward her office door. A cup of coffee, or better still some hot soup, would revive her. She hadn't had any breakfast, and no dinner last night; it was no wonder she felt so weak.

She opened the office door, intending to ask Sara if she could bring her back a carton of soup from the nearest sandwich bar, only to discover the outer office was empty. Of course, both girls would be having their lunch. She would have to go herself.

Her office was on the fifth floor, and by the time she reached the ground floor via the lift she was beginning to wish she had never left it. Gritting her teeth, she walked uncertainly across the foyer and out into the penetrating cold dampness of the lunch-time streets.

Surely they were not normally as noisy as this? The heightened sound battered against her aching eardrums. She had to blink several times to bring things properly into focus. The sandwich shop seemed unpleasantly hot after the coldness of the street, her head pounded and the rich scent of hot food made her stomach churn sickly.

The queue moved slowly, but at last it was her turn to be served. At first she couldn't remember what she wanted. Those behind her in the queue shuffled impatiently, and miraculously her mind cleared. Soup.

She ordered it, and found she had to hold the carton carefully because she was trembling so much.

Outside again in the street she shivered violently. Was it her imagination or had the temperature dropped several degrees while she had been inside the sandwich bar?

It seemed to take her for ever to hobble back to her office building. Her ankle felt as though it was on fire as it swelled protestingly against the confinement of her leather boot. How on earth she was going to get the thing off she had no idea. The thought of not being able to do so and having to wear it for ever struck her as very funny, and she started to laugh, but her chest went tight and she couldn't breathe. She stopped abruptly and someone cannoned into her, knocking the soup carton out of her hand.

A long, expensive scarlet car drew up at the kerb. Kate didn't notice it. She was too busy mourning the loss of her soup.

A hand gripped her arm, a familiar voice said her name peremptorily, and then fell silent, causing her to lift her head in mute query.

For some reason it didn't strike her as particularly odd that Rick should be there, just when she had been thinking so despairingly of him, and wishing she had not been so stubborn when he had urged her to go home. Had she done so, she could by now have been tucked up in bed, fed and warm.

Half out of her mind with fever, she looked at him without surprise and said piteously, 'I dropped my soup.'

And fresh tears welled.

She heard Rick curse and then, so abruptly that she grabbed hold of him in shock, he picked her up, and carried her over to the car, easing her gently into the passenger seat.

'Don't you dare move,' he warned her. 'Which floor's your office on, Kate?'

'The fifth, but there's no one there.'

He wasn't listening, though. He was already half-way across the pavement. It was sheer bliss to simply lie back in her seat and let someone else take charge; she was even beyond being appalled that she should feel like this. She was beyond everything but giving in to the fever consuming her.

When Garrick returned she was lying with her eyes closed, her pale face stained along the high cheek-bones with a brilliant scarlet flush. As he got into the car he checked her pulse and found that it was racing erratically.

She opened her eyes and looked at him, her clear gaze for once glazed and unfocused.

'I'm hot,' she told him in a small, bewildered voice. 'I don't feel well.'

'I think you've got 'flu,' Garrick told her curtly. 'I'm taking you home, Kate, and then I'm going to call your doctor, and if you dare to tell me once again that there's nothing wrong with you, so help me . . . I'll . . .'

'Michael——' Kate protested drowsily.

'I've managed to persuade one of your neighbours to keep an eye on him for an hour.'

'How did you know that I needed you?'

Had she been fully in control of herself, there was no way those words would ever have been said, and with her eyes closed she was not aware of the brief betraying look he gave her. She might admit that she needed him now, but were he to remind her of those words when she was well again, he suspected that she was all too likely to deny ever having said them.

What had started out as a simple ploy to gather enough information to make sure that a court would award him full guardianship of Michael had turned into something far, far more complicated.

And the worst of it was that he could see no way free of the tangle of deceit he had wound around himself. As he drove over a rut in the road, Kate gave a small moan and he switched his attention from his contemplation of abstracts to the reality of the woman seated next to him.

CHAPTER NINE

FOR Kate, the next twenty-four hours passed in a haze of confused events: their return home, Rick undressing her and putting her to bed, despite her feverish protests, the arrival of the doctor who agreed with Rick that she was suffering from a severe bout of 'flu. The doctor added to Garrick, although Kate herself wasn't aware of it, that she suspected Kate was also under a considerable amount of strain, which wasn't going to help her recovery.

She woke several times from the heavy sleep that claimed her, each time worrying fretfully about Michael and the office, only to be told by Rick that everything was under control and that she wasn't to worry, but over a whole day elapsed before she was able to ask him for concise details of exactly who was taking care of Michael while he sat at her bedside.

'I got in touch with one of those twenty-four-hour emergency services. They sent round a relief nanny. Oh, and they've also arranged for someone to go into your office and deal with the day-to-day routine stuff while you're off.'

'You've what?' Kate shrieked, sitting bolt upright and then groaning as her head started to pound. 'Have you any idea what those agencies charge?' she protested bitterly. 'Rick, I can't afford to...'

She heard him curse under his breath, his hand cool as he placed it against her burning forehead. She was shivering again now, and desperately weak, only too glad to give in to his firm instruction that she lie down again. It was wonderful to lie there and be cosseted, to have the bedding pulled up and tucked round her as her mother had done when she was a child; to have someone telling her not to worry and that everything would be all right, and her mind, already clouded with fever and fear, readily abandoned its anxieties to Rick, as he soothed her and told her she was not to worry.

Garrick sat with her until she had drifted back to sleep, and then he stood up with a frown. He wouldn't be able to fob her off so easily for very long. She was no fool. The temporary nanny was costing the earth, and of course he was footing the bill himself; as for her office, he had instructed Gerald to send someone suitable there, to take charge of the everyday basic things, so that the two girls would be left free to take over Kate's own workload. He had warned Gerald that whoever he sent must be discreet and capable of holding her tongue, but once Kate was back to normal . . .

He looked down at her sleeping form, marvelling a little that she should have the power to move him so deeply. The problem was, did she reciprocate his feelings? There was a physical awareness between them, there was no doubt about that, no matter how much Kate might shy away from it, but would she be prepared to change the course of her life, to deviate from the route she had mapped out for herself to include him in her life?

It gave him encouragement and hope that she had done so once—to include Michael. He grimaced faintly to himself. He loved her. He who had always sworn that he would never commit the folly of falling in love had proved to be just as human and vulnerable as his fellow men, and he didn't mind at all.

What he did mind was the fact that he was daily deceiving her, that she had a totally erroneous view of him. How would she react when he told her the truth? He would have to wait until she was well, of course. Patience had never been one of his strong suits and he hesitated in the doorway, reluctant to leave her, and yet knowing that sleep was exactly what she needed to aid her recovery.

It was over a week before Kate, who in the early feverish days of her illness had insisted that she was going straight back to work, felt strong enough to get out of bed for a couple of hours a day, and sit with her feet up, listening to Michael's gurgles and staring lazily into space.

She was now in the recuperative stage of her illness, her doctor informed her, adding severely that it was going to be at least a month before she was anything like fully fit.

'And even then I have my doubts about whether you're going to be strong enough to go back to work. You've been pushing yourself too hard for far too long,' she had added gently. 'It can't go on. If you knew the number of young women who are coming to me with all the hallmarks of tension and stress. I'm all for sexual equality, but I sometimes wonder if we shouldn't concentrate on making the male of the species more like us than vice versa.'

The temporary nanny was no longer required, for which Kate heaved a sigh of relief. Every now and

again when she allowed reality to penetrate past the
lazy barrier of self-protection engendered by her
illness, she was pierced by a sharp and frightening
awareness of how perilously close to financial disaster
she must be.

And her doctor was right about the strain she was
under. She found herself increasingly reluctant to even
think about going back to work, and that terrified
her. Instead of looking forward to it, she found that
she was deliberately pushing it to the back of her mind.

It was as though losing James's contract and then
her bout of 'flu had robbed her of all her old ambition. She was quite content to allow Rick to take
messages from Sara that all was going well and that
she was not to worry; she felt no burning urgency to
find out for herself what was happening in her absence, and every now and again, like lightning piercing
heavy dark clouds, she was rent by panic as she realised how easy it had become to simply allow herself
to drift aimlessly from day to day, allowing Rick to
take control and organise her life for her.

When she eventually brought herself to confide
these fears to her doctor, the older woman smiled
grimly and said, 'As I've already tried to tell you, too
much stress. This is your system's way of telling you
that it's had enough.'

'But I must get back to work. I can't simply sit here
and drift.'

'If you don't listen to what your body's telling you,
you could well find yourself on the verge of either a
heart attack or a nervous breakdown within a very
short space of time,' her doctor told her bluntly. 'What
you're feeling now is just a warning, Kate. I can't force

you to heed it, but I can tell you that if you don't, you're all too likely to be far more seriously ill in the long run.'

'But you don't understand,' Kate fretted, and then went silent, knowing that she could not confide her financial fears to her doctor.

After she had gone, she sat tensely in her chair, desperately trying to think of a way out of her problem. When her bedroom door opened and Rick came in with Michael, they brought with them the coldness of the outdoors.

'Five times round the park and we've fed the ducks,' Rick told her with a grin, tossing Michael up in the air, much to the little boy's delight.

There was a bond between them that tugged at Kate's newly tender heart-strings. Watching as Michael trustingly allowed Rick to throw him up again, her own emotional response to the sight of them, the big strong man and the small, vulnerable, trusting child, brought a hard lump of anguish to her throat.

This was how life should be: a traditional family unit, two loving adults bonded together by their care of the child life had entrusted to them.

'What's wrong?'

The quiet words hurt her with her knowledge that they were simply an expression of social concern, with none of the deep-rooted and intensely personal caring she longed for.

The unspoken words tolled through her mind, shocking her into abrupt realisation of the truth.

Somehow...somewhere...she had done the unforgivable and she had allowed herself to become dependent on Rick. Feverishly she searched her mind, trying to push the unwanted knowledge to one side, trying to convince herself that she was wrong, that it was simply her weakened state that was causing her to have these thoughts, but she knew as she looked at him that when the day came for him to leave them her life would be emptier than she had ever dreamed it was possible for it to be.

Somehow or other her heart had turned traitor on her, and he and Michael had become fused together in it as two permanent features in her life.

He reached out and touched her, concern pleating his forehead into a frown as he put Michael down and turned his attention to her.

'What's wrong, Kate?' he repeated worriedly. 'Aren't you feeling well?'

Her skin burned beneath his touch, her pulses thudding tensely and the knowledge burst upon her like a shower of too bright light.

She loved him.

The knowledge hit her with the appalling severity of a mortal wound. She went pale with the shock of it, the blood draining from her extremities like a death flood, and she stared blankly at him, unable to think logically or say a single coherent word.

'Kate, what is it?'

The rough warmth of his voice was like an abrasive powder ground into too tender skin and she flinched from it, terrified of the swift surge of need within her to cling to it and to him. She went hot and cold and her body shook, and it was a hundred, no, a thousand times worse than the 'flu.

'Kate...'

He was actually touching her now, holding her shoulders, cupping the smooth round joints in the palms of his hands, and it seemed to her in her heightened mood of awareness that his fingers actually caressed the silk of her skin, but she knew she was simply thinking that because she wanted to think it.

She drew a deep gulping breath of air, trying to steady herself. She mustn't let him guess what was wrong with her; she shrank from the fool she would make of herself if he were to realise. She, the dedicated career woman, desperately in love for the first time in her life.

'I'm all right,' she lied.

'No, you're not. What is it? Something the doctor said?'

She seized on the excuse gratefully, nodding.

'She's right, you know,' he told her, shocking her with the realisation that her doctor must have discussed her physical condition with him. 'You have been over-straining yourself. I know how desperate you are to get back to work, but you aren't well enough yet.'

His compassion overwhelmed her. She bent her head to hide the sudden, stupid rush of tears to her eyes and was shocked to hear herself admitting huskily, 'That's just it. I don't want to go back.' She drew a deep, shuddering breath, and tried to move away from his constraining hands. When he touched her she could barely think straight; her whole body yearned toward him, aching wantonly for his touch. She could feel the now shockingly familiar coil of painful need tense her stomach, and she ached to press herself against him, to be wrapped in the hardness of his arms.

She looked past him towards the window and said more to herself than to him, 'What's happening to me? I scarcely recognise myself any more. Why do I feel like this? I ought to be eager to get back to work. Instead . . .'

'It's called post viral depression,' Rick told her gently. 'A common occurrence with 'flu victims, especially when they've been as ill as you've been. I know that doesn't make it any easier to bear, but it will pass, I promise you.'

'How can you say that? You don't know . . .'

'Yes, I do,' he contradicted her. 'Three years ago I suffered a similar experience. It was the most demoralising thing I've ever known. But I promise you there is life after 'flu,' he told her teasingly.

Life after 'flu, yes. But life after him—never.

The realisation that she loved him kept her tense and restless when she ought to have been concentrating on recouping her strength. She slept so badly for two nights and looked so frail and drawn on the third night when he brought up her dinner tray, he insisted that she was to drink all of the large glass of rich red wine he had poured for her.

'But I don't like it,' she protested. 'It goes straight to my head, especially red wine.'

'Think of it as medicinal.'

Until she'd realised that she loved him, Kate had been having her evening meal with Rick. Since then she had cravenly insisted on eating alone in her room, and she had seen from the expression in his eyes that her refusal to share the evening with him puzzled him.

She shrank from his classing her with his previous employer, the woman whose sexual advances had led him to handing in his notice. How well she could understand that woman now. She shivered, despite the warmth of her bedroom, and Rick frowned.

She was not recovering as fast as she should. He privately considered that she would recuperate far more quickly somewhere warmer. He thought of the villa in Corfu bought half on impulse, half as an investment and now so rarely used, but there was no way he could suggest that she stay there without alerting her suspicions.

Kate watched him as he placed her dinner tray on the small table. In the early days of her recuperation, she had marvelled at the delicacy and variety of the meals he brought her to tempt her appetite, and he had confessed to her that they weren't his creation but had been delivered via a special restaurant service he had found in Yellow Pages.

Kate had winced at the thought of how much it must be costing, but when she had tried to point this out to him he had told her bluntly that his own cooking skills were not such as would tempt the appetite of an invalid.

Tonight there was chicken breast in a delicate cream sauce, flavoured with some sort of spirit, although she couldn't recognise which one, accompanied by delicious new potatoes, no doubt flown in at great expense, and a tempting variety of beautifully cooked and arranged vegetables. For pudding there was a very special egg custard, again beautifully cooked and arranged in a pure fruit sauce to add piquancy to its flavour.

But as she ate it, and reluctantly drank the wine Rick had brought her, Kate knew she was not doing justice to the delicious food.

The double burden, not only of her love for Rick, but also of her growing reluctance to face up to the reality of what the loss of James's contract was going to mean to her business, was haunting her, sapping her strength like an invidious disease, leaving her wan and listless when she ought to have been getting better. Sometimes she even wondered if she was deliberately sabotaging her own recovery, just so that she could bask for a little longer in the warmth of Rick's cocoon. Once she would have scorned such an idea, but now... Now she was no longer sure if she knew herself at all.

When Rick returned with the bottle of wine and insisted on pouring her another glass, she demurred, but he poured it anyway and left it on the table beside her bed, saying that she might feel like it later.

He offered her coffee, but she refused, knowing that even the smallest stimulant was likely to keep her awake into the small hours of the morning as she fought to come to terms with what was happening to her.

She sensed that Rick wanted to stay and talk. On previous evenings, before she had realised what was happening to her emotions, she had enjoyed their discussions, finding in Rick a male companion intelligent enough to challenge her, and at the same time confident enough of himself to accept her fully as his equal. She missed their verbal sparring, but that was nothing to how she was going to feel once he had gone from her life completely.

She fell asleep thinking about him, and then woke up abruptly at two o'clock in the morning to find the covers had slipped off the bed, as she struggled restlessly in her sleep, and she was freezing cold.

Pulling on her robe, she went to check on Michael, wondering if a sound from him had woken her, but the little boy was deeply asleep. She touched his smooth soft face and felt an unfamiliar urge grip her body. What would it be like to conceive the child of a man one loved? To carry that child and eventually give birth to it ... the strongest bond there could be between two people who loved.

She was shaken by the tempest of emotion that swept her, leaving her shivering and achingly aware of how barren her life was going to be. She would never sleep now ... and she wondered how long she was going to be condemned to spend the hours of darkness tormented by her thoughts of Rick.

She half stumbled back to her own room, and saw the glass of red wine. That should warm her, and help her sleep too. She picked it up and drank it quickly, as though it was medicine, pulling a wry face as the full-bodied claret slid down her throat.

There was more in the glass than she had imagined, and even before she had finished drinking it she was conscious of the sudden burst of warmth heating her stomach. On an empty stomach and in her tense, nervous state, the intoxicating effect of the strong wine was almost immediate.

She could see the room blurring almost in front of her, and when she tried to get into bed, to her bewilderment, the bed seemed to shift hazily in front of her, as though it was a floating mirage and not really material at all.

She clutched hold of the quilt to steady herself, and found to her astonishment that she was sitting on the floor with it. She started to giggle, the whole situation suddenly unbearably funny, but somewhere along the line her giggles changed to tears and she started to cry, uninhibited, wrenching tears of intense pain.

The noise woke Rick, who had learned to sleep lightly in case Michael called out during the night and disturbed Kate. At first he couldn't place the alien sound, and then he realised that it came from Kate's room, not Michael's, and he was on his feet, tugging a robe over his nude body. He hadn't worn pyjamas since he was a child, and although he had attempted to do so to soothe Kate's outrage, he had found them so constricting that he had soon abandoned them.

The sight of Kate huddled on her bedroom floor, clutching her quilt, her face streaked with tears, made him think that she had had an accident. He rushed over to her, demanding quickly, 'Kate, what is it? What's wrong? Is it your ankle?'

Her ankle had healed, the bruised swelling disappearing, but it was still liable to give way at odd moments.

Before she could say a word, he was touching her, his long fingers investigating the delicate bone, one hand supporting the slimness of her calf while the other probed delicately around the ankle itself.

Heat radiated upwards from where his hand touched her skin. Her heart was pounding unevenly, her body gripped by a wanton, urgent need, crying out to her so loudly for satisfaction of that need that it drowned out everything else, including the warning voice that begged her to remember her dignity and her pride.

Rick's head was bent over her ankle as he frowned his concern. Unable to stop herself she reached out and touched him, her fingers trembling as they rested, fluttering against the hard angle of his jaw.

He looked at her.

'I want you to make love to me.'

Too late now to recall the betraying words. Her whole body burned with humiliation and despair. What on earth had made her say them?

'Kate . . .'

He said her name softly, reaching out to take hold of both her wrists and gently push her away from him. She could see the rejection in his eyes and she flinched from it and from herself, burning with self-mortification. No matter how kindly he rejected her, they would both know that he had done so. Why hadn't she held her tongue? Why had she . . . ?

'I'm sorry. I don't know what made me say that. It must have been the wine,' she gabbled, desperate to ease the tension filling the room. She saw that Rick was about to speak, and, unable to endure hearing his denial of her, rushed on frantically, 'I didn't mean it, Rick. I know how you feel about female employers who come on to you. Please forget what I said. I . . .'

'Forget it? I can't do that, Kate.'

Something had changed; the deep timbre of his voice told her that. Where he had been about to gently reject her, where he had been firmly pushing her away from him, his fingers were now slowly caressing the thudding pulses in her wrists, and the dark glow in his eyes was not that of an unaroused man.

The wine had gone right to her head and she barely knew what she was saying or doing, he knew that. By rights he ought to put her to bed and leave her there, but he had seen in her eyes her belief that he was rejecting her, and he cursed the ill fortune that had decreed that the man whose place he had usurped had left his previous employment because of the sexual harassment of the woman of the house.

He was caught in a double trap and he knew it. If he left Kate now, she would think he was rejecting her, and he knew her well enough to know that once she was completely herself again, she would make sure that there would never be another opportunity for him to break through her defences. Her pride would ensure that.

And if he stayed then she would probably accuse him of taking advantage of her when she was too ill to know what she was doing. He was damned either way; and if he was going to be damned, he knew which of the two memories he would rather take with him.

For too many nights now he had lain in that too narrow and almost too short single bed, on fire for the feel of her in his arms, aching with a torment he could remember experiencing even during his teens, his body pulsing hungrily with its need for her.

A more sexually experienced woman would have recognised that need and probably exploited it, but Kate seemed to have no awareness of her effect on him. Hence the look of anguished rejection in her eyes right now. A look he would give his soul to extinguish. A look he could wipe away simply by taking her in his arms and letting her feel how very wrong she was when she assumed he didn't want her.

'You should be in bed,' he told her huskily.

He stood up, taking her with him, and holding her against his body, securing her there with one arm, while he picked up the quilt with the other. The movement hardened the muscles of his belly, and Kate was pressed so closely to him that she could feel it, her own stomach quivering in arousal at being so close to his strength. Still holding her, he tugged the quilt back on to the bed. Kate found that her head seemed to nestle of its own accord in the curve of his shoulder.

She wasn't sure if Rick was simply remaking the bed for her benefit, or...

'I don't think I'm going to need this, do you?' he whispered against her hair, releasing her briefly to shrug off his robe.

'I forgot my pyjamas again,' he added throatily, sliding her own robe away from her body, and then bending his head to nuzzle the scented skin of her throat as he eased down the shoulder straps of her nightdress.

'Rick,' she protested huskily.

His mouth had reached the curve of her jaw.

'Shush... Don't talk now. Kiss me instead,' he murmured against the corner of her mouth, and the movement of his lips sent wild vibrations of sensation coiling through her.

'Rick——' she protested again, but more weakly this time, wild panic seizing her as his lips slid between her own, parting them and then caressing them with ever-increasing passion.

She didn't know when she started to kiss him back, or when he released her arms from the straps of her nightdress to allow it to slide to the floor so that he could gather her body into his arms and slowly caress the length of her spine as he urged her into the waiting heat of his own flesh. It was all so new, this sensation of flesh against flesh, this closeness, this intimacy, and yet it was also as though part of her had known it since the beginning of time.

She stopped kissing him, drawing back in his embrace to search his face with a fevered gaze. 'Rick, I've never done this before. I don't want to disappoint you...'

'You couldn't,' he told her gently, drawing her back against him and tracing the outline of her mouth with his tongue, distracting her from what she knew she ought to say.

Beneath his breath he muttered rawly, 'If anyone's going to be disappointed, it could be you. I want you too much right now. Feel,' he whispered softly, his hands moving down her spine to hold her against him. 'Feel how much you arouse me, and promise me that no matter what the future holds, you'll never doubt how much I want you...'

Kate hesitated uncertainly, sensing the tension in his words, groping towards understanding what might lie behind them, but Rick demanded urgently, 'Promise me, Kate. Promise me that *no matter what happens*, you won't allow anything to destroy these memories.'

His fingers dug into the tender softness of her bottom, and she sensed that he wasn't even aware of the pressure he was exerting. He breathed deeply and his body moved against her own, sending sharp spirals of desire coiling through her.

'I promise,' she told him unsteadily, marvelling at the darkness of his eyes and the faint tremor of his hand as he brushed her hair off her face. Then, holding her shoulder, he kissed his way along her throat and down over her body until she was arched willingly and wantonly over his arm, as instinct and arousal demanded that she focus his attention, both mental and physical, on the feminine perfection of her breasts and their dark crowns of yearning flesh.

She trembled as his mouth moved moistly on her, caressing the soft swell of pale skin, his hand cupping her other breast. Then his fingers began caressing its taut peak, until she quivered and shook and wondered with agonised impatience why he didn't know how tormenting it was to have his mouth moving so delicately on her smooth, pale skin, when what she wanted . . . what she needed . . .

'Rick,' she protested huskily, and immediately he stopped caressing her, lifting his head so that he could look into her eyes.

'What is it? Don't you like that?'

'Yes. No. Rick, I want . . .' Her heart thundered and pounded within her chest, the words locking in her throat, her eyes darkening with her need to have his mouth against her flesh.

And then, as though he knew that she could not endure the torment any longer, his gaze dropped to the dark peaks of her breasts, and she felt his breath graze tormentingly against them as he said fiercely, 'Is it this that you want, Kate? Is it?'

And he drew the sensitive nub of flesh into his mouth, caressing it with his tongue, and then, when she cried out, he suckled fiercely first on one and then on the other nipple. As though the soft cries of pleasure muted in her throat drove him beyond the edge of his self-control, his palms cupped the outer curves of both breasts, gently pushing them together, so that his mouth could move swiftly from one pulsing pleasure point to the other with a rhythmic urgency that seemed to flow from his body to her own, so that she was not quite sure when the thrusting hardness of his body's possession was no longer merely her fevered mind's hungry fantasy but actual reality.

The feel of him inside her went beyond any pleasure she could imagine there could be; even the brief locking of her muscles as they felt the thrust that broke the final barrier was in some odd way a painful pleasure, willingly endured for the delights that came after it.

'I'm sorry, my love, but this time I can't be temperate,' she felt Rick whisper against her mouth as the tempo of his possession increased.

He groaned against her mouth and savaged it with biting kisses as passion overcame him. Kate felt the tiny, beginning ripples of it, but as she reached out to capture the sensation Rick cried out and she felt the hot pulse of his climax.

'I'm sorry. It was too soon,' he told her, still holding her in his arms, but strangely she felt no disappointment, only a vague ache and an intense feeling of tiredness. She badly wanted to go to sleep and she curled up against Rick, burrowing into the warmth of his body.

By rights, he ought to go back to his own bed. What had happened already was bad enough, but if he stayed here with her there could be only one outcome to the enticement of her soft, naked flesh against his own.

He was right. Towards dawn Kate was woken by the most delicious of sensations she had ever experienced washing slowly through her body, and by the time she was awake enough to realise that it was caused by the soft caress of Rick's mouth against first her stomach and then her inner thigh, she was too aroused to do anything more than cry out in a torment of shocked pleasure that convulsed her body and turned her weak with sensation as Rick's tongue gently traced the most secret intimacy of her sex. Then his mouth caressed her until she was mindless ... lost ... adrift in an ocean of pleasure, no longer caring if she sank or swam.

Nothing in her life had prepared her for the explosion of pleasure that shook her, nor for the astounding speed with which Rick was able to make her reach out for that same pinnacle of pleasure again as he told her thickly, 'That was for you. This is for both of us. Something for both of us to cherish.'

In the false dawn she saw a muscle beat in his jaw, and wondered at the bleakness in his eyes. He was as grim as though he was a condemned man, but her body, awash with delight, refused to allow her mind to concentrate on anything other than the physical delight he was giving her.

The quivers of her first climax had barely died away before she felt his mouth on her breasts, teasing the hard nipples into aching points of desire. She felt the arousal of his body, moving urgently against her and then within her so strongly that she felt she would die from the pleasure she was experiencing.

This time the pleasure was stronger, fiercer, the convulsive grip of her muscles locking on Rick's body making him groan and shake with arousal, and then for a few fleeting heartbeats they were no longer human, but immortal, spinning dizzily into space together, and the music of the universe rang in Kate's ears as they heard Rick's harsh cry of fulfilment and she knew that it was her body that had given it to him. The sensation she felt at the knowledge was so primitive, so female, that the force of it shocked her.

CHAPTER TEN

'THERE'S a phone call for you. A Camilla Lancing.'

'Camilla? Oh, lovely, I'll speak to her.' Carefully avoiding looking directly at Rick, Kate picked up the receiver.

It had been three hours now since she had woken up to the realisation that she and Rick had been lovers; three hours, during which she had battled frantically against her panic that he might guess that for her last night had not just been the emotional whim of the moment, but a lifetime commitment.

In the cold light of the dark November day, she was all too aware of how irrationally and idiotically she had behaved. She didn't regret that she and Rick had been lovers; how could she? But what she both dreaded and feared was what she might have betrayed to him through her actions.

Discreetly he left the room while she spoke to her friend.

'Who on earth was that?' Camilla asked her, obviously intrigued, once Kate had asked after her father-in-law and been assured that he was now well on the way to recovery.

'You should know,' Kate responded as light-heartedly as she could. 'You were the one who recommended him. He's Michael's nanny.'

There was a small silence, and then Camilla said, 'Kate, are you well enough to have visitors? I'd like to come round and see you.'

Kate was dressed and sitting in her room. 'Lovely. I've rather a lot to talk to you about.'

Too proud to ask for any direct help, she would nevertheless be grateful for the opportunity to talk over her fears for her business with her friend.

Camilla arrived half an hour later. Rick let her in on his way to the park with Michael. Kate heard them exchanging 'hellos' as they passed in the hall.

Kate greeted her friend with a smile, but there was no answering smile on Camilla's face as she walked into the room.

'Kate, what's going on?' she demanded without preamble. 'And please, no more fairy-tales. The day Garrick Evans needs to hire himself out as anyone's anything is the day the business world turns topsy-turvy... What *on earth* is he doing here?'

Kate stared at her in shock.

Rick Evans. Garrick Evans. Why on earth hadn't she made the connection? Why on earth hadn't she guessed? Garrick Evans, Alan's remote second cousin. Garrick Evans, who had announced to her via her solicitor that he wanted nothing to do with his second cousin's child.

She sat numbly while Camilla's rueful expressions of remorse went past her unregarded. A feeling of terrified panic, not unlike that experienced during the most traumatising of nightmares, possessed her; she felt as though she had strayed into an unknown world without any signposts to guide her. A feeling of physical sickness engulfed her, and she started to shake as she tried to understand why Garrick Evans was living in her home, pretending to be Michael's nanny.

Michael. Suddenly all her fears coalesced and focused on one thing... Michael. Michael was the key to this. He had to be. Michael was the reason that Garrick Evans was here, that he had lied to her, that he had played a cruel charade with her, that he had inveigled his way into her home, her bed... her life, under totally false pretences.

'You didn't know, did you?' Camilla apologised. 'Oh, Kate, I'm so sorry.'

'Where did he go?' Kate demanded tersely, ignoring her apology. 'I've got to get up. He's got Michael with him. Oh, God, how could I have been so stupid? I've got to find him.'

'Kate, no. You're in no fit state to do anything. Please tell me. What's going on? What's he doing here? How can I help?'

'You can't,' Kate told her dully. 'No one can...'

They both heard the front door open and then close again. Michael's laughter floated upstairs, accompanied by the deep tones of Garrick's voice.

'Do you want me to stay with you?' Camilla asked, sensing that Kate intended to confront him with the truth.

'No!' She shook her head. 'No, thanks.'

What was going to happen would be painful in the extreme, and she wanted no witnesses to it, no matter how sympathetic and kind. It was bad enough that she had betrayed herself so stupidly, without others witnessing her humiliation.

God, how he must have laughed at her! Garrick Evans...superstud par excellence. No wonder he had known exactly how to... Her mind cut off then, refusing to go any further down such a hurtful path.

'I'll go, then,' Camilla said awkwardly, seeing that Kate was hardly even aware that she was still there. 'I'm sorry, Kate. Perhaps I shouldn't have said anything, but I knew that the man who was supposed to come for the interview had taken another job, and I was worried.'

'No... no. You did the right thing,' Kate told her slowly. 'It's better this way...'

And, seeing the look in her eyes, Camilla did not ask her what it was exactly that was better.

She passed Garrick on the stairs. He had Michael in his arms and stood back to let her pass. He noticed her set face, and the way she avoided his eyes, and the vague feeling that he had met her somewhere before became certainty.

He swore softly under his breath. He had planned to tell Kate the truth today, knowing that he could not allow himself to go on deceiving her now that they had been lovers.

He put Michael in his playpen and then opened Kate's bedroom door. The moment he saw her face, his suspicions were confirmed.

'You know, then,' he asked calmly.

'That you're Garrick Evans?' She gave him a tight, hard smile. 'Yes, I do. I suppose Michael's at the root of this whole charade.'

He had known she was intelligent and keen-witted, but even so her percipience startled him. It deserved the only honest reply he could give her.

'Yes,' he told her bluntly. 'But, Kate...'

'You've got half an hour to collect your things together and leave. And just to make sure you do, I'm going to call the police.'

She was actually dialling the number, he realised, and he had no doubts that she meant exactly what she said.

'Kate, we have to talk,' he protested, but she wouldn't look at him, fiercely punching out the numbers into the telephone.

He bent down and tugged swiftly on the connecting flex, disconnecting her.

'Let me explain.'

'What?' Kate demanded fiercely. 'Why you lied your way into my home...my...trust...my...my bed?'

She couldn't add 'my heart', but it was what was hurting her the most; that and her fear that somehow or other his presence threatened both her and Michael.

'The deceit was accidental, not calculated. If you cast your mind back, you will remember that *you* were the one to assume that I had come for the job of Michael's nanny.'

'You could have corrected me.'

He acknowledged her comment with a grim frown.

'I could have, but at the time it seemed an ideal opportunity to have a chance to get closer to Michael, to collect the evidence my solicitor told me I would need to get a court to hand him over into my care.'

He saw her go white, and ached to take her in his arms and tell her how he felt about her, but she was like a terrified cat, ready to attack friend and foe alike in her panic.

'So I was right,' she hissed. 'Michael *is* what all this is about. *Why?* Why do you want to take him from me? You had the opportunity to accept your share of responsibility to him when Alan and Jennifer died, but you rejected it. I still have the letter.'

'My solicitor wrote that without my authority while I was out of the country,' he told her calmly. 'And before you say anything, I can prove it.'

'Just as you can prove that you'd make a far better guardian for him than me? Because you've got more money, more power, more everything... I suppose that's why you went to bed with me, isn't it?' she added in a high voice, her whole body shaking with the force of her emotions. 'So that you could prove to the court how unfit I am morally as well as financially. What did you do, Garrick? Make notes to pass on to your solicitor... record...'

She was working herself up into a state of acute hysteria, and he could hardly blame her. There was only one way to stop it. He walked over to her and yanked her out of her chair, binding her protesting body to his own.

'Stop it, Kate,' he reinforced when she tried to claw at him. Her eyes were wild, like those of a hunted animal, her face pale except where her cheekbones were highlighted by patches of hectic colour.

'You're wrong. Oh, I admit that when I first came here I was hoping to get enough evidence against you to prove that I was more fit to have guardianship of Michael than you. You see, I'd reached that point in my life where it was beginning to come home to me that I've worked myself into the ground for nothing... or rather, for no one... and the thought of an heir, a son...who could be had without the encumbrance of a mother whose role in my life I did not want either outside or inside marriage, was a very alluring prospect indeed!'

He saw her face and smiled grimly.

'I'm paying you the compliment of being totally honest with you, Kate.'

'Isn't it a bit late for that?' she countered bitterly.

'I hope not, but only you can know the answer to that question. You're looking at a man who's been converted to a view of life he's never previously wanted to see. I'm a very successful man, Kate, and without being vain or boastful that success has meant that I've never been short of female company and admiration, but just as someone working in a sweet factory grows to loathe the very sweetness of the confectionery they make, so I found I was rapidly growing very disenchanted with the female sex. Greedy, grasping...shallow.' He saw her face and grimaced. 'Yes. I know how it sounds, but I'm trying to be honest with you. You see, knowing you has opened up a whole new vista to me. I see life and my place in it in a way I never have done before.'

'You mean you've realised that women can be gullible fools, easily convinced by an experienced liar?'

'No! What I mean is that I believe that Michael needs both of us in his life. No one could love him more than you do, Kate, but you must admit that it's difficult for you trying to cope with building up a new company and the day-to-day problems of caring for a small child.'

The very reasonableness of his argument struck a fresh chill in her soul. What was he going to do? Offer her money to part with Michael?

'Kate, we're both people who've made a decision to live our lives alone. Both of us have decided that commitment, permanency...a lifelong partner are not for us. I suggest that we should think again.

'I've learned a lot living here with you. I've learned for instance that it's possible for a man to find a great deal of pleasure in caring for a child . . . even a small child, and I've also now a much clearer insight into how difficult that kind of caring can be . . . how tying and at times how tiring. I've also learned that there are women who are vastly different from those with whom I've sometimes shared my life, and I blame myself for the fact that I've only just learned this. Call it a self-defensive practice, if you like, but that's what I believe it was.'

He felt the tension in her body and sensed her desire to break away from him.

'What I'm trying to say, Kate, is that instead of fighting over who should have Michael, why don't we join forces and share the pleasure and responsibility of bringing him up?'

'A week with you and then a week with me, do you mean?' she demanded brittlely. 'Turn and turn about.'

'Not exactly.' His eyes narrowed as he looked down into her angry face. He could feel the stubborn resistance holding her body taut, and he knew that this was going to be far harder than he had hoped. 'What I had in mind was something a little better than that. I want to marry you, Kate.'

Her body suffered the shock of it . . . the awful pain and despair of being given so much and so little.

'Because of Michael?' she asked him bitterly. 'No, I'm sorry, Garrick. You may be enjoying a different vision of how you see your life progressing, but I'm afraid I don't share it. I want a career, not marriage.'

She broke free of him and walked over to the window, keeping her back to him. She didn't want him to look into her face and see how much she was suffering. She had to convince him that she couldn't marry him. To be married to the man she loved simply for the sake of a child in whom they both had an interest . . . No, that was something she could not and would not endure. She had her pride.

'I see.'

How silky and menacing his voice sounded.

'A career, you say. Doing what, Kate? Working for someone else? Because that's what's going to happen, isn't it? You barely have enough funds to keep your business going another two months. You badly need new contracts. You . . .'

'*You've* had my business investigated? How dare you? What were you trying to prove? That I'm financially incompetent? Well, I can soon change that . . . All it takes is one phone call to James. Of course, I'll have to sleep with him to get his business, but what does that matter now? I . . .'

'God, Kate, no!' Garrick interrupted her explosively. 'Turn your back on me if you must . . . hate me even, if you want to . . . but please don't sell yourself to someone like Cameron. It would destroy you. If the company is so very important to you, I'll give you some business. I've already . . .'

'Thanks, but no thanks. What is it, Garrick...guilty conscience perhaps? I've gone to bed with you, therefore I have to be paid off, just like your other women?' Kate demanded recklessly.

'Is that what you really think?' His mouth twisted. 'I suppose there is a certain kind of rough justice that you should. Listen to me, Kate, because whatever else you may or may not choose to believe about me, this much is true. I didn't want to make love to you last night. I knew it would only add to my burden of deceit.'

Kate went ashen.

'There's no need to remind me that I was the one to proposition you, Garrick,' she said proudly. 'But...'

'For God's sake woman, will you allow me to finish just one sentence? I didn't want to make love to you because I knew it wasn't the right thing to do, not with all that you didn't know about me, but I couldn't stop myself... I've spent too many nights lying awake, aching for you, to be strong-willed enough to deny my need.'

He reached for her and wordlessly she let him take hold of her. Holding her, he traced the trembling outline of her mouth with his thumb, brushing the soft curves tenderly.

'Is this because you hate me?' he asked her softly, undermining her defences. 'I love you, Kate. I didn't mean to... I certainly didn't want to, but I do, and although you may think it arrogantly male of me, I think you love me too. No woman could make love the way you did last night and not care. I fully intended to tell you the truth today, I promise you...and to ask you to be my wife, and not because of Michael.

'The first time I walked into this house, all I could think of was how convenient it would be to have a child without the inconvenience of its mother. Michael himself meant nothing to me, I admit it. But you changed all that. I love Michael. I can't deny it, but that's not why I'm asking you to marry me.'

'I'm a career woman,' Kate protested huskily. 'I wouldn't make you a good wife, Garrick. Not the kind of wife a successful man like you needs to run his home and bring up his family.'

'Wrong,' he told her forcefully. 'You're exactly the kind of wife I need. The only woman I could ever want as my partner through life. And marriage to me doesn't mean you must abandon your career, Kate. In fact, I wouldn't want you to. It may not be easy at times for either of us, but with luck . . . with sheer hard work . . . and most of all with love . . . we can make it.'

'Can we?' Kate sighed, no longer able to resist him.

'Let me prove it to you.'

She quivered wildly as his mouth touched hers, unable to deny herself the bliss of holding him, of touching him, of letting his mouth convince her of all that he had already said.

A career . . . a husband . . . a family. It sounded too good to be true.

As though he knew what she was thinking, as he released her, Garrick said huskily, 'I can't promise you that you'll have it all, as they say in the books. No one does! To imagine that they do is a fallacy. Compromises will have to be made, but I think that any amount of compromising is worth while if it makes it possible for us to be together. I want you as my wife, Kate. I want that more than I've ever wanted anything in my life. We go together, you and I. I know you need and want your career, and I don't want to stop you having those things. Marry me and I'll prove it to you.'

She looked at him and he added rawly, 'I'm not going to beg you to trust me, Kate.'

'You don't have to,' she told him softly.

He was strong, this man of hers; strong enough to allow her to be her own person, to accept that she could not devote her life to living in his shadow. As he had said, it wouldn't be easy, but somehow they would find a way to make it possible, feasible, viable. After all, they had the strongest bond there was. Their love.

'So!'

Kate picked up her telephone and punched out the number of Garrick's private line.

'Are you free for dinner with me tonight?' she asked him once she had heard the familiar tones of his voice.

'In what capacity?' he teased her. 'As my wife...or as the director of my PR agency?'

'Neither,' Kate told him with a smile. 'And don't bother asking any more questions. It's a surprise.'

As she put down the receiver she grinned delightedly to herself. In fact, it was two surprises, and she intended to save the best until last.

Only this morning she and Camilla had agreed the final details of the deal that would make them equal partners in the new PR company they intended to form. With Camilla as her partner, both of them would be able to afford to split the responsibilities of running the business. It was rather like job-sharing with a difference, Kate chuckled, and she was also going to be the first to benefit from the new partnership because in eight months time, just in time for their first wedding anniversary, she would be presenting Garrick with their second child. A brother or sister for Michael.

Was it only just over six months ago that Garrick had cautioned her against expecting to 'have it all'? She smiled again. Her life came as close to perfection as it was possible to come.

The M4 motorway made it possible for them both to commute daily to their offices from the pretty Queen Anne house they had bought just outside Bath.

Michael had settled down well with his new nanny, an older woman who seemed to know just how to deal with children; and he had also taken to his adoptive grandparents in the shape of Garrick's mother and father.

Kate herself was getting to spend more time with him than she ever had before, since she had been able to promote Sara to office manager, and now there was the new partnership with Camilla and their mutual agreement that they would take it in turns to work from home, using the advanced computer technology Kate's recent success had made it possible for her to buy.

Garrick had helped her there, giving her as much of his many companies' PR work as she could handle. And it wasn't nepotism, he had been quick to assure her. He had been impressed with the presentation she had prepared for James, and he continued to be impressed with the work she did for him.

'The results speak for themselves,' he had told her when she had demurred that other members of his main board might not look too kindly of him giving so much PR work to his wife and a company that was still only just getting established.

But she had proved herself now, and the success of the campaign she had introduced for Garrick's companies had drawn other businesses to her. She and Camilla had agreed that they would keep the business small enough for them both to handle, because, as she had discovered these last six months, there was more to life than mere material achievement, much . . . much more. And she hugged to herself the knowledge of the pleasure Garrick would take in learning that they were to have a child.

Having it all? Maybe not from the viewpoint of the woman she had once been, whose career had been everything to her, but these last six months had taught her that, if she had to lose everything else, so long as she still retained Garrick's love she would have all that she could ever want.

She glanced at her watch. Another five hours before she met Garrick for dinner. She couldn't wait to see his face when she told him their news.

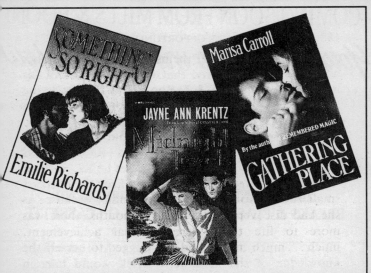

COMING SOON FROM MILLS & BOON!

Your chance to win the fabulous

VAUXHALL ASTRA
MERIT 1.2 5-DOOR

Plus

2000 RUNNER UP PRIZES OF WEEKEND
BREAKS & CLASSIC LOVE SONGS ON CASSETTE

SEE
♥ MILLS & BOON BOOKS ♥
THROUGHOUT JULY & AUGUST FOR DETAILS

AROUND THE WORLD WORDSEARCH
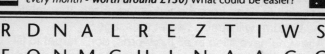

How would you like a years supply of Mills & Boon Romances ABSOLUTELY FREE? Well, you can win them! All you have to do is complete the word puzzle below and send it in to us by October 31st. 1989. The first 5 correct entries picked out of the bag after that date will win **a years supply of Mills & Boon Romances** (*ten books every month - **worth around £150***) What could be easier?

```
R D N A L R E Z T I W S
E O N M C H I N A A C C
G M U I G L E B N N U O
Y E C E G W H I Z C B T
P D R H S E R I A Z L A
T N S M P E R U N D D A
N A W I A T P I I E N N
Y L A T I N A N A N A D
N G S T N H Y D E M L Q
W N O J A M A I C A L A
R E L A D A N A C R O R
T H A I L A N D D K H I
```

ITALY	THAILAND	SCOTLAND	SWITZERLAND
GERMANY	IRAQ	JAMAICA	
HOLLAND	ZAIRE	TANZANIA	
BELGIUM	TAIWAN	PERU	
EGYPT	CANADA	SPAIN	
CHINA	INDIA	DENMARK	
NIGERIA	ENGLAND	CUBA	

PLEASE TURN OVER FOR DETAILS ON HOW TO ENTER ➡

HOW TO ENTER

All the words listed overleaf, below the word puzzle,
are hidden in the grid. You can find them by reading
the letters forward, backwards, up or down, or
diagonally. When you find a word, circle it or put a line
through it, the remaining letters (which you can read
from left to right, from the top of the puzzle through to
the bottom) will spell a secret message.

After you have filled in all the words, don't forget to fill
in your name and address in the space provided and
pop this page in an envelope (you don't need a
stamp) and post it today. Hurry - competition ends
October 31st. 1989.

Mills & Boon Competition,
FREEPOST,
P.O. Box 236,
Croydon,
Surrey. CR9 9EL

Only one entry per household

Secret Message _____

_____

Name _____

Address _____

_____

_____

_____ Postcode _____

You may be mailed as a result of entering this competition

COMP 6